TOO HOT TO HANDLE

A CURVY GIRL ROMANCE

RIVER LAURENT

Too Hot To Handle

978-1-911608-21-9

ACKNOWLEDGMENTS

Thank You

Brittany Urbaniak
&
Peggy Schnurr

CHAPTER 1

MADISON

"Oh, come on, you know it's going to be fun!"

"I'm just not sure," I rolled my eyes at my best friend, Eleanor, who was sitting opposite me with a look on her face that told me she was never going to take no for an answer.

"It's precisely what you need right now." She nudged my foot with hers beneath the table. "A bit of fun, yeah?"

"I think it's more fun for you than for me," I said, taking a sip of my coffee and shaking my head.

She leaned back and observed me for a moment, before letting out a long sigh, obviously trying to figure out how she could best twist my arm. "Well, since I'm right off of a break-up." she nodded pointedly. "I get one wild night on the town with you, no questions asked, right?"

"I guess so." I finished my coffee and fiddled with the sugar packets on the table in front of me, arranging them in parallel lines. "It just doesn't sound like my kind of thing, though."

"What? Hot guys aren't your kind of thing?" She was the one rolling her eyes now. She reached into her bag and pulled out a slightly crumpled brochure, and laid it out on the table in front of me, smoothing out the creases.

"What are you, their PR person now?" I teased.

She waved her hand enthusiastically at me. "Just look at this guy," she said as she stabbed her finger onto the paper. "Chad Weston. How can any woman with blood running in their veins not want to see him in person?"

"That leaves me out. I have coffee running in mine."

She sighed elaborately as if I was too much for her to put up with. I looked down at the man she was pointing to. Okay, I had to admit, he was swoon-worthy hot. Well, they were hardly going to put some plain guy on the front of the brochure advertising their male strip show, were they? Even so, his bright green eyes and mess of brown hair were cute, and that big-ass grin was almost as distractingly attractive as his ripped abs and muscular arms.

"I guess he's pretty hot," I shrugged.

She threw her hands dramatically in the air, attracting the attention of a few people sitting around us. That wasn't a problem for her. She liked attention, loved it when she was the center of attraction. *"Pretty hot?"* she squealed. "Do you know they call him Subway Chad."

I frowned. "Subway Chad?"

"Don't play coy. Haven't I seen you eating their twelve inch sandwiches before."

I flushed bright red. I knew that was a little dig at my weight too. "Oh, that."

She smirked. "Yes, that. Don't you agree it will be worth seeing? You've never seen one that big have you."

I swallowed hard. Now I was certain everyone was looking at me as if I was some kind of freak. "No," I croaked.

"So, you're going to come with me?"

"I don't know, El."

"Come on. The boys are only in London for a couple of days more. It's their last show and our only chance to see him."

I shrugged. "It's really not my thing."

"What would you do otherwise. Bury your face in one of those ridiculous books of yours?"

I bit my lip. That was exactly what I planned on doing. "What's your game-plan? Just look at him until you get over Jonathan?"

"Nope," She grinned widely. "I'm going to get that American dude into my bed. It's my life work."

"What, ever since you saw this brochure, you mean?"

The sarcasm was lost on her. She nodded. "Ever since."

"So you down for it?"

I gave a long sigh. I guess it wouldn't kill me to go out with her for one night. "What time does it start?"

"Seven, and I promise you won't be disappointed," she said nodding at me pointedly. "You never know you might get to go home with one of the other men in the troupe."

"I don't think so," I fired back immediately.

"Why not? It'll just be a one night stand. You know, just let yourself go with a perfectly gorgeous God of a man."

I was not the kind of girl men who looked like that would chose to take home for the night. I carried a bit too much weight around my hips and thighs and I had the kind of face you would miss in a crowd. I was a plain Jane. In all probability I would be taking a taxi home on my own, which actually suited me just fine. "I'll come by your place and meet you at half-past six."

"Not necessary. I've got the transport all sorted out. I'll come pick you up at half past six." She got to her feet, and leaned in to drop a quick kiss on the side of my cheek. "Come on, we need to go and get you a dress."

"I have plenty of dresses," I protested. "I don't need any more."

"Trust me, what you have at home isn't going to do it for an event like this," She pulled me to my feet. "We're going shopping."

CHAPTER 2

MADISON

"Fine," I got to my feet reluctantly. Hanging out with Eleanor these days left me feeling more exhausted than ever; she was always running around, dragging me to this and that, as though just my company alone wasn't enough for her anymore. Now that she had split with Johnathan who she had been with for almost a year, I had to come to terms with the fact that I was going to be seeing a lot more of her than I had been before. In the past she tended to get obsessed with dudes, getting stuck on them at the expense of nearly everything else in her life and needing me to offload on, but at least with this stripper, Chad what's-his-name, he would be out of the city by the end of the night.

Although, I had to admit, I was a little cynical about her chances of hooking up with him, anyway. How many women must throw themselves at him all the time? I mean, Eleanor was beautiful, with slim hips, a wasp waist, and bee-stung lips that seemed to have men falling at her feet, but this guy got women hot for a living. It wasn't like he could be short on them.

"Oh, I'm so looking forward to this." She was practically prancing down the street as she peered into the windows of shops we passed by, to find something that looked good on me. I really didn't want to get anything new, but if it would make her happy and help get her mind off the break-up, then I wasn't sure I, as a best friend, was allowed to argue. Even though it often felt as though we'd gone in different directions these last few years, I still felt this sense of duty towards her.

"Ooh, what about that one?" She pointed at a blue dress in the window of a shop I knew just by looking would be way out of my price range. The dress looked pretty good on the mannequin, but I wasn't sure how it would go on me – the deep blue was a pretty color, and I liked the sweetheart neckline that looked smart and not too over-the-top. Like something I could wear to work.

"I guess we could give it a go," I replied gamely, and we headed in to try it on.

The shop was part of a big shopping center. There was a bookshop sitting next to it that I glanced longingly over at. God, if I could just duck in there for five minutes… I never regretted blowing a big portion of my paycheck on books, even if my sister always mocked me for it. Not that I had much of a paycheck these days, the company I'd done sales for two years just shut down last month. That's part of the reason I didn't want to drop all this money on a dress, or on tickets for this show tonight. I didn't have it to spare. But I would do what I had to, to help Eleanor.

"Come on, try it on!" she urged as soon as she'd found a version of the dress in my size.

I took it from her and slipped into it in the changing rooms, trying not to look at myself too closely in the mirror. It wasn't that I hated my body or anything. No, I just didn't find much use for it these days. I hadn't dated anyone in a long time, and, not being one for one-night-stands, that pretty much meant that I hadn't had sex for a very long time. Also, I had put on some weight. I knew that my hips were wider and my thighs softer than they had been before. It bothered me enough to want to try and pretend it wasn't happening.

I looked up once the dress was zipped around me, and I twisted back and forth in front of the mirror while I tried to figure out whether I liked it or not. It certainly wasn't *bad*. The blue popped against my dark hair, and it cinched in a few bits of me that needed it, but it wasn't precisely *good* either. It just sort of *was*.

"You dressed in there?" Eleanor called, and before I could reply she had whipped the curtain back. She looked me up and down and nodded slowly, as though this was exactly what she'd had in mind.

"Yeah, that's perfect," she grinned up at me. "Don't you think?"

"Uh, it's okay," I nodded. "Not…not really much, to be honest."

"Once you're all done up for going out you'll feel different," she promised with some authority. "You should definitely buy it."

"You think?" I asked doubtfully.

"For sure," she replied firmly.

I glanced down at the tag hanging off the hip and winced once more. The tickets for this place were going to be expensive too, I knew that, and then there would be the taxi there and back and the overpriced drinks at the venue...

"Stop worrying," Eleanor clicked her fingers in my face, pulling me back to the real world. "It's all going to be fine, alright?"

"Alright," I conceded.

Shooing her out of the dressing room I took another look at myself in the mirror. Yeah, I guess the dress looked okay. I had seen myself look better, but that was before I put on all that weight. Also, I just wasn't used to seeing myself dressed up. It had been more than a month since I'd had to go into the office with anything resembling a nice outfit on. Most of these days, I sat around in my apartment in jeans and a baggy sweatshirt, reading and cooking and jumping every time the phone rang in case it was someone wanting to offer me a job interview. It never was.

The job market was as rewarding, it seemed, as the dating one.

I bought the dress and watched as the saleslady carefully folded it in tissue before slipping it into a bag. Fortunately, the one pair of heels that I owned were black and would go with it.

Eleanor was practically skipping along beside me, she was so excited about the rest of this evening. It was starting to get dark, the light leaching from the sky, just like the hope that I had any chance of getting out of this event which was about as far removed from 'me' as it could possibly be.

"I wonder what he'll be like in bed," she wondered, like it was just a matter of time before she found out.

I bit my tongue to keep from pointing out to her that this hook-up wasn't a given quite yet. If she wanted to have her little fantasy no good would come for me to shit all over that. I just smiled and nodded along. Might as well get used to it. I was going to have to listen to that for the rest of the night.

CHAPTER 3

MADISON

An hour later I was back home. I dropped the bag with my new dress on the sofa and trudged over to the shower, figuring that I might as well start getting ready. But, just as I switched it on, there was a knock on the door. Wrapped in my towel I hurried over to the door. It could only be my sister.

"Sasha," I greeted with a smile.

She stepped over the threshold to my place without saying a word. She nodded at me, the straps of her handbag held in her teeth as she rooted through her pockets for something. When she was done, she plucked the leather handle from her mouth and gave me a massive grin.

"Hey," she gave me a quick hug, and then zoomed in on the bag I had dumped on the sofa. "Ooh, what's that?"

"I got a dress for going out tonight," I explained, and she opened her mouth, her eyes lighting up, but I held my hand up to stop her before she got too excited. "Eleanor's dragging me out to this male strip thing," I rolled my eyes. "She says it's to help her get over the break-up, but she's just trying to hook up with the lead dancer."

"Oh," Sasha wrinkled her nose up. "Doesn't sound much like your kind of thing."

"It's not." I shook my head at her. "But she's going through a break-up and I want to help her out, you know?"

"And where was she when you split up with...what was his name?" Sasha called over her shoulder as she headed into the kitchen to make herself a cup of tea. She was the only person who could get away with just turning up at my house and treating it like she owned the place.

I followed her into the kitchen. "Yeah, okay, whatever," I said following her into the kitchen and waving my hand at her. I didn't want to think too hard on the fact that she was right. Eleanor hadn't been there for me when I'd split up with my ex, Frank, eighteen months ago. She just didn't deal well with the big dramatic stuff, she'd told me, and she'd been convinced that what I needed was time and space to heal myself. I was sure what I needed was support from my best friend, but I was too gutted to do much more than loll around the apartment feeling sorry for myself.

She started to fill the kettle. "Do you want a cup?"

I shook my head.

"Let's get a look at this dress, then." She put the kettle on and herded me back to my small living room. "See if I can spin my magic and make it fit you better."

"Okay, let me get into it." I quickly threw on the dress once more, and spread my hands out and did a twirl. "What do you think?"

I saw the furrow in her brow before she could cover it up. "Hmmm...." She pressed her lips together.

"It's not good, is it?" I muttered, my suspicions confirmed as I plucked at the blue fabric of the dress. It was hard to see if something really suited you in those narrow mirrors shops had in the changing rooms. Now I was sure the dress made me look like a beached whale.

She shook her head and got to her feet, and began to rummage in her handbag.

"What are you looking for?" I asked, walking over to the full length mirror I had in the hallway. God, I looked huge.

"I'm seeing if I have my sewing kit with me," she replied absently, and then I heard her go, "Aha!"

"Do you think you can rescue it?" I asked, shifting back and forth in front of the mirror.

"They don't call me golden fingers for nothing at work."

I glanced at the clock. "I don't have that much time, though. El is coming to pick me up at six thirty."

"You go for your shower." She waved her hand airily. "Leave this thing with me. I'll have it looking fantastic in no time."

"You don't have to-"

"But I want to," she cut me off firmly, the way only she could. She waved her hand again. "Come on, you, out of here."

I did as I was told. I headed straight through to the shower to get myself looking passable for the evening. There were serious upsides to having a sister who worked as a dress-maker, not least the almost magical power she had of turning the worst, most hideous clothes into something really special.

I got out of the shower, blow-dried my hair into soft waves down my back, then I applied mascara and lipstick the best way I knew how. I emerged from the bedroom in my bra and panties and saw Sasha putting the finishing touches on the dress.

"Wow!" I exclaimed, with widened eyes. The dress was practically unrecognizable.

She glanced up at me with an excited grin, the same one she always had on her face when she knew that she had pulled something big off.

"I knew when I was looking at it that there was something special in here somewhere," she blurted out, talking quickly. "The color suits you so much and the cut was good, it just needed a little coaxing. Anyway, try it on. Be careful with the stitching, it's a little delicate."

"Yeah, just what I need, the whole thing coming apart in front of a crowd full of people," I teased, but took the dress gingerly from her and looked down at it. A big grin passed over my face as I looked up at her.

"Thanks for this," I murmured. "It really means a lot to me."

"I'm not letting my little sister go out on the town looking like crap." She got to her feet. "I'm a dressmaker, how would that reflect on me?"

"Fair point," I conceded.

"Now, hurry up and get it on. I'm dying to make that cup of tea I never had."

CHAPTER 4

MADISON

I slipped the dress carefully over my head and Sasha zipped me into it.

It fit like a dream. I could tell that before I even looked at myself. I thought it had fit well enough before, but this was the difference between a dress that could get over my body and a dress that actually enhanced what I had on show.

"How do I look?" I asked.

She smiled. "Go see for yourself."

I walked over to the mirror and my jaw dropped.

She had cut a low neckline into the dress, low enough that I seemed to have magicked up a huge dollop of cleavage from nowhere. She had nipped the dress in around the waist because it made it seem as if I actually had a waist. She had taken up the hemline too. It now came down to just above my knees, and the way it clung to my thighs was borderline scandalous. Well, one thing was for sure, she had effectively made it impossible for me to use this as a work dress. There

was no way I was going to be wearing this to any job interviews anytime soon. Unless it was for a very specific type
of job.

I twisted back and forth in front of the mirror, taking myself
in, and then finally stepped into my only good pair of heels
that I owned, black and with a bow that tied around the
ankles. Okay, I actually looked pretty good. A smile spread
over my face as I looked myself up and down, and I tried to
remember why I didn't get dressed up to go out like this
more often.

My sister beamed at me. "You look fantastic."

"You think?"

"Absolutely. I don't know why you don't dress like this more
often instead of slouching around in those shapeless things
you wear." She came over and started fluffing about with the
hem. "I knew I could do something with this thing. You
really do look amazing, Madison."

I gave her a quick hug. "Thanks for this. I really needed this
tonight."

"Yeah, I can imagine," she replied, and I knew immediately
she was referring to Eleanor. She had never much liked her,
but I tried not to let it get in the way of my relationships with
either of them. I told myself Sasha was just protective, but
sometimes I wondered if there really was something in
Eleanor she needed to protect me from.

Sasha went off to make her tea and I spent a little more time
preening myself, making sure my lipstick was perfect and
throwing back a bottle of water to make sure that however
much I had to drink tonight it wouldn't leave me with too

brutal a hangover the next day. A couple of minutes before half six, there was a knock on the door.

"Oh, that'll be Eleanor." I jumped to my feet, and wobbled on my heels and had to catch the arm of the sofa. God, I was just not good at these dangerous things. I could have broken my neck back there.

I buzzed her in, and opened the door to find myself face to face with Eleanor in her full-glamour mode. She looked damn good, in a short, sparkly silver sheath dress that was practically blinding me even in the dim lighting of the hall outside my apartment. Add to the fact that her heels were high and her hair was teased out and huge, it made her virtually impossible to miss, even from miles away. Which would be a good thing, if she intended to catch the eye of the Subway guy.

The only thing that wasn't shining about her was the frown marring her forehead as she cast her gaze over me. I felt my mouth go a little dry as she looked me up and down.

"What's the matter?"

"Your dress," she blurted out.

"Don't you like it?" I struck a pose playfully, but she didn't seem overly amused.

She brushed past me and into the apartment. "Is that the same dress?" she asked, crossing her arms over her chest. There was that furrow in her brow again, letting me know that somehow I'd done something wrong.

"Yeah," I nodded, and pointed to the kitchen where Sasha was still rumbling about. "Sasha did a little work on it for me. I think it looks nice. Don't you like it?"

"It just looks a little…" she trailed off, giving me a long look up and down once more.

Sasha emerged from the kitchen, and her lips tightened when she saw that Eleanor was already there.

"It just looks a little tarty, that's all," she finally finished up, and I felt my cheeks flood with heat at her words.

"I can go change into something else," I suggested, my chin dropping in embarrassment.

"I think you should. Go on then. Quickly."

"No fucking way," Sasha said firmly, shooting some serious daggers in the direction of Eleanor. "You look fantastic, and I worked too hard on that for you not to go out in it now."

"Fine," Eleanor sighed, tossing her hair over one shoulder as though this was the biggest inconvenience she could imagine. "You don't have time to change anyway, the taxi's already waiting outside."

I gave Sasha another quick hug. "See you soon, okay?"

"I'll lock up before I leave.," she replied, throwing another venomous glance at Eleanor. "Have a good night."

Her words were barbed even if they seemed innocent, and I knew that they were aimed at Eleanor and not me. I got where she was coming from. Sometimes, I felt as though I wanted someone who called herself my friend to treat me with a little more respect, but I knew that she had been through a lot these last few weeks so I couldn't expect too much from her.

We headed out to the taxi.

CHAPTER 5

MADISON

Eleanor wasn't saying much, eyes fixed on some point out the window, not bothering to even glance over at me. I tugged the hem of my dress down and frowned. Was it because I had gotten all dressed up? Did she think I looked better than her or something? I couldn't help but wonder if she'd been so enthusiastic about that dress because she'd known that it was quite dowdy and would make her appear even more splendid, but now that I'd actually turned the heat up a little she didn't like it one bit. Which kind of surprised me, how could I steal her thunder. She was by far more attractive than me.

We arrived and picked up the tickets that Eleanor had booked on-line. I looked at the price on my ticket and gulped. That could feed me for nearly two weeks. She must have bought the best tickets in the house. We headed towards the entrance doors. The foyer was packed-out with people, the vast majority of them women, and the place was crackling with a tension that I wasn't sure I'd ever felt before in my life.

"Holy shit, this place is packed," I yelled to Eleanor over the sound of the crowd.

She glanced over at me and finally a smile appeared on her face, and I felt a wave of relief hit me, as she seemed to actually be having a good time after all.

"Yeah, well, he's not going to see anyone but me," she replied, pointing up to the enormous billboard that showed off a giant, blown-up picture of Chad Weston. His eyes were lowered to the ground, but his body spoke for itself, and I felt a little flutter in my chest as I took him in. I had never been one for guys who were hot in that really showy, obvious way but he was...hell, he was something else entirely, and I had to admit it was doing it for me.

We were jostled around on our way to the front of the queue, but finally, we made our way into the theatre and took our seats. Even in the dark, the place was bathed with a warm pink lighting that made my heart beat a little faster. It looked like we were heading for the front row. So he could see Eleanor, no doubt, or at least that had to be what was going through her mind.

"Are you sure about this?" I asked Eleanor again, suddenly nervous for what was about to come.

She glanced over at me, brow furrowed with annoyance. "Of course, I am. Come on, sit down, you're in everyone's way."

I took my seat and my heart fluttered when I realized that he would likely be able to see me, too, and I was suddenly glad that Sasha had worked her magic on this dress. I wanted to look good tonight, wanted to look really good, wanted to look better than anyone had seen me before.

It must have been the atmosphere pulsing through the room that had me thinking that way, because I had never felt anything like it before as long as I'd lived. It was like a hen night turned up to twenty, to a thousand times more intense. All these women talking and giggling and occasionally bursting out into little shrieks of excited laughter, as though they could barely keep inside how badly they wanted this. I glanced over at Eleanor, smiling, hoping that she would give me some of that same connection, but she was sitting there staring at the stage with a slight frown on her face. She was probably coming up with a game plan inside her head that didn't include me. I glanced around at the groups of friends laughing and talking and knocking back gulps of their cocktails, and wondered where I had gone wrong that I was missing out on that part of the evening right now.

Suddenly, the house lights lowered, and Eleanor tapped excitedly on my knee, then cupped her hands around her mouth and let out a long whoop, one that blended in with all the rest of the noise coming out of the audience. The excitement in the air was palpable, and I found my heart start beating faster too. I was actually getting into it and couldn't wait to see what this evening had to bring.

"Ladies..." A loud, cheesy voice boomed from the speakers around the venue. "Welcome to...The Man Up Project!"

The rest of what he was saying was drowned out in a series of shrieks of excitement, and I had to grin as the curtain ran up and revealed the men waiting for us behind it. There were at least a dozen of them. I didn't have the time or inclination to count, but they were all moving as though they were in total and utter control of their bodies, totally calm, totally controlled, totally, totally, totally hot. And all of them were stripped to the waist, showing off their insane bodies, sculpted abs and strong arms and bulging pecs.

I scanned the stage to see where the leading man was hiding himself, but I couldn't make him out.

Maybe they saved him for later. It was hard to focus, given the music pulsing out of the speakers and the noise of the crowd. Most of them were on their feet, but Eleanor was still sitting down, as though she hoped that being different might be what attracted the attention of the Subway fame, when he finally arrived, that was.

Still, I wasn't going to sit around having a miserable old time just because she wasn't ready to have fun yet and, taking even myself by surprise, I got to my feet and began swaying my hips back and forth a little to the music. It felt good, really good. There was a whoop from right behind me and I turned around to find the woman in the seat behind ours giving me the thumbs-up. I grinned and flashed her the same sign back. Then I quickly turned my attention back to the stage where the men were dancing, in perfect harmony to the same pulsing beat of the retro dance track that was blasting out over the speakers.

That song came to an end, and the stage was dipped into blackness once more; the audience quieted, as though sensing that something good was about to happen.

At last, when the atmosphere in the room could be cut with a knife, he emerged.

CHAPTER 6

MADISON

There was no need for me to squint to second-guess who he was. Even without getting a proper look at him, I knew this had to be the main man. The lights were so low that I could barely make him out, but he had this presence about him. The way he strode onto that stage through the piles of men in front of him let everyone in that theatre know that he was the one in charge, that it was him they needed to watch out for.

As he stood there on stage, I stared at him, taking him in, unable to tear my eyes away from him. He was fully-dressed but somehow, despite the gorgeous half-naked men around him, he was the only thing in the world that mattered to me and, for a split second, I was sure I saw him looking back at me.

My heart jittered to a stop in my chest as our eyes met.

Then he lowered his gaze once more, just as he did on the poster, and took his position at the center of the stage. The moment was broken, that moment that had passed between us, where I had been sure that there had been that flicker of something real and raw and divine in that look he gave me.

The silence around the room continued for another long moment. Then, as the lights came up, so did the noise. I realized that I had been holding in a breath, and let it out with a long gasp.

His head snapped up and he faced the crowd for the first time, and the women's screams reached crescendo pitch. The atmosphere in the room was incredible, indescribable. Even Eleanor got to her feet. I supposed the sight of him here in real life in front of her was enough to get her to forget any games she might have had and just go for it.

The way he moved was something different from the rest of the guys who had opened the show. Sure, they hit their marks alongside him, just the same way he did, but he oozed a kind of unique confidence and charisma, the kind of thing you couldn't learn with practice. He moved his body like he knew how much everyone in that room wanted him, something that I couldn't relate to. I had always felt a little out-of-place in my own body, and I longed for the kind of confidence that he seemed to own so effortlessly.

Eleanor moved like she was starting the seduction right there and then, and I pressed my lips together and tried not to judge her too harshly for it. She had just been through a break-up, after all, and I shouldn't take whatever she was going through too seriously. Everyone needed some space to relax and blow off some steam. Maybe even me.

After the first song was done, the lights fell low again, the only spotlight was on him. I grinned up at him from where I was standing, and I was sure that he looked down at me once more. I felt myself flush a bright red as soon as his eyes were on me, and embarrassed I glanced away at once. There was just something unbelievably erotic about having him look at me like that.

"Now..." he spoke into his mic. His voice was deep and sexy, and another series of shrieks went up from the audience around me. He seriously owned this place, and he had barely been on-stage for three minutes.

"Put your hand up if you don't want to come up on stage with me tonight," he grinned, casting a look around the audience. I looked around and saw only about a dozen hands in the whole place that went up, from friends who looked as though they'd been dragged here by someone else. I bit my lip and returned my gaze to the stage, and there he was, looking down at me again.

"Because I'm going to need someone to come up here and give me a hand." He looked over the audience once more. Another cheer raised the roof.

"Who's going to help me?"

Pretty much every single woman in that room seemed as though she would have been happy to volunteer, and I whooped right along with them, letting him know that I was very much in their midst. He lifted his finger, letting it rove over the crowd, and then, to my utter shock—

It came to rest on me.

I stood there and just stared at him for a moment. No. Out of all the women in this room, there was no way that he was pointing at me. I glanced over at Eleanor, and I instantly figured out from the foul look she was giving me that yes, he really was pointing at me.

"In the blue dress down there," he announced, smiling directly at me. "Get up here, Gorgeous."

Me gorgeous. Did he just call me gorgeous? I continued to just stand there, peering up at him as though I had no idea what he was asking me. And then, I felt a nudge in my side. The woman next to me, a big smile on her face, was pointing to the stage.

"Go on you lucky thing, get up there!" she ordered me. I forgot about Eleanor glowering beside me. I beamed and grinned and blushed and finally did as I was told. The crowd whooped me along, and I felt as though my feet weren't touching the ground.

I blinked in the bright lights of the stage, feeling like I had been caught out in the light of a million searchlights, but then I felt his arm slip around my waist and everything else in the room dropped away.

CHAPTER 7

MADISON

"And what's your name?" he asked. He was looking out on to the crowd and engaging everyone in the room, but at the same time, I felt as though I was the only thing there that mattered to him. My toes curled in my heels as I inhaled his sweet scent; he was wearing an expensive aftershave, something deep and masculine and musky, and I wanted to bury myself in it and never come out.

"Madison. Madison Brooks," I replied softly, looking into his eyes. They were so blue and so bright, even more so than they'd seemed from my seat. The way they glinted at me made something light up deep in my stomach.

"Madison," he repeated, and the crowd hollered once more. "Good to meet you, Madison. You ready to help me out?"

"Yeah," I bit my lip, a bit embarrassed, and grinned at him, and I noticed that his thumb was tracing along my waist a little. Did he do this with everyone he brought up on stage?

One of the men he'd been dancing with pulled out a chair from backstage, and placed it down in the spotlight. The light spread and softened as Chad guided me down into the seat, pushing me gently until I was sitting down and staring up at him. He was practically naked in only a pair of under-wear, and I could see the shape of his very generous cock even through the fabric. Subway indeed. He leaned in close to my ear, his breath hot on my cheek, and I licked my suddenly dry lips, and tried to keep my cool.

"Just let me know if anything gets too much for you, okay?" he murmured close to my ear, and I knew those words were just for me, and oddly it felt intimate. As we were about to do something sexual and not take part in a performance on stage.

"I will," I promised with a nod, and he drew away and turned back to the crowd, the moment between us dropping away as the music lifted once more.

"Are you ready?" he yelled out to the crowd.

They replied in the affirmative so he turned back to me, and straddled me.

I felt as though my brain had dropped out the back of my head. I gulped as his hard thigh muscles brushed lightly against my body. Then he looked directly into my eyes and I thought I was going to die. Oh, god. This man was something else.

The whole time that he was using me to dance around and against. At first, I felt a little self-conscious up there on stage, in front of all those people, and being the object of desire for the sexiest man I'd ever met, but then, as I got used to sensa-tion of his hard body gyrating against mine, I forgot all of that and focused entirely on the way he made me feel.

It was impossible not to.

The way he touched me, going slow at first with the beat of the song, pushing a strand of hair back from my face, and leaning in close to my neck, his mouth so warm and so close and so tantalizing, I was finding it hard to keep my head straight.

And then, as the music picked up, he began to really move. He flexed his hips and ground against me, his eyes boring into mine, a slight smile playing at the corner of his sensuous, full lips as though he knew precisely what he was doing to me, and had no intention of letting up. I knew he'd told me that I could stop this whenever I wanted, but no part of me wanted for it to end. No, I wanted more and more.

The song spanned on, but I could barely hear the music any longer, or the screaming of the crowd. In fact, I couldn't concentrate on anything else in the room, but the sound of his breath and mine mingling in the air between us. I could feel my pulse picking up, my body reacting to the way that he was moving on top of me, around me, behind me.

Jesus Christ, I was getting wet!

Standing behind the chair, he slipped his hands down my waist, and hooking his head over my shoulder. I closed my eyes and wondered how obvious it was that I was getting turned on, but I didn't care who saw it. Part of what was getting me off was knowing how sexual he was being with me in front of all these people. I wondered how far he would take it. I wondered how far I would let him…

Because I didn't want to stop. Ever.

The song came to an end, with him right up in my face, only

a few inches away from me. He was breathing a little heavily and so was I. I could have sworn I saw his eyes flick down to my mouth for a moment like he was thinking about kissing me right there and then. I tilted my head up, letting him know that I wouldn't have turned it down. He lingered for a moment longer before he seemed to reluctantly pull himself away.

"How about that?" He raised his hands once more and the sound of the crowd began to filter into my brain once more.

I blinked. For a second there when it looked like he was about to kiss me I had forgotten I was up on stage. God, the way he had looked at me. The audience cheered and whooped, and I wondered how many of them were sick with jealousy that I was the one up there and not them. I couldn't see Eleanor's face but I had a feeling she was going to be pretty fucking pissed that he had chosen me and not her.

"How about another one?" Chad asked, and there was another wave of screaming agreement from the audience. He turned to me, with a grin on his face, and shrugged as though he couldn't disappoint his fans. He raised his eyebrows at me, silently asking if this was okay, and I nodded at once. I realized my lips were a little parted, like I had been getting ready for the kiss that had never quite come.

"Wait for me," he said, and ducked backstage. He returned with something in his hand, and pulled me to my feet. My legs were still so wobbly that I found myself falling against him for support. Thank heavens he was there to prop me up because otherwise I swear, I would have crumpled to the ground in a heap in front of everyone. His body felt so good, so hard and strong next to mine. Without thinking I tentatively laid a hand on his chest. And I didn't even feel slutty.

CHAPTER 8

MADISON

He took a seat in the chair, then guided me in close so I was standing between his legs. I bit my lip and looked down at him. Surely, he didn't expect me to dance for him this time. Or did he? Because I had two left feet and no way was I going to humiliate myself in public.

Thank God, dramatically, and in one strong motion, he pulled me on to his lap. The audience went crazy. I had to catch my breath as I fell on top of him. My arms slipped around his neck. I couldn't quite believe that this was happening to me, but I felt his cock pressing into me through the thin fabric of my dress. Suddenly I was filled with a deep craving to slip my fingers beneath his boxers and just take him in my hand and then…

"You want more?" He was addressing that question to the audience, but it was also a question for me.

I nodded at once. There was no way I could have said no at that point. He could have suggested that the two of us have full sex up on that stage in front of everyone, and I would have gone for it. I just wanted to feel him, to feel every inch of him, to take as much of him as I could in one go.

He lifted his hand and revealed that he was holding a can of whipped cream. Needless to say the crowd went crazy. My eyes widened as he handed it to me.

"You want a taste?" he asked.

It took me a moment to realize what it was he was suggesting. He closed his fingers around mine and guided the can to his broad chest. As I stared at him dumbfounded, he raised his eyebrows at me expectantly. Finally, it sunk in.

I took the can and tentatively drew a line of cream down his chest; my eyes were drawn to the rippling muscles there, to the sheer strength of him. I wondered what he could do to me with that kind of power.

And then, feeling bolder than I'd ever felt in my life, I leaned in and licked the cream off his chest. The crowd was hollering, perhaps imagining themselves in my position, or maybe just entertained by how bold I'd suddenly become.

Underneath the cream, I could taste him.

I had never thought about how a man tasted before this, but I could taste him right there, and something about his taste got me really hot all of a sudden. I had been turned-on before, but this was something else, something more.

I placed my hand on his chest and felt the beat of his heart and realized that it was most probably going that fast for reasons other than the crazy dance routine he'd just performed. I looked up at him, my tongue still trailing over his chest, and widened my eyes at him playfully. His hand came to the back of my head as he looked down at me. If he

RIVER LAURENT

had guided my head downwards I would have gone with it. No complaints and no problems at all.

Once I had taken care of that thin line of cream, I went to put another over his stomach, a little lower down, hungry for him now and uninterested in holding back my desires. I bit my lip as I drew the line down, closer to his underwear than before, and I might have been crazy, but I was sure I could see his cock stirring to life beneath the fabric. I wanted to touch him down there so badly, but I also didn't want to do anything that might get in the way of me being up here. I had no idea what the rules were, but I had a feeling that straight-up getting down on my knees and licking his dick would probably be a little too far.

The neckline of my dress had inched down a little, and I noticed his eyes straying down to my cleavage. Oh, he could have those babies any time he wanted. I leaned down, and let my tongue trail along that spot below his belly button, that sensitive part that made his chest jerk up suddenly. The crowd was screaming their encouragement, and I loved how in-control I was right then. He had been the one in charge at first, but he hadn't counted on me being the one to go this far. It had been a long time since I had actually felt this kind of desire and there was no way in hell I was going to pass up the chance to act on it now that I had been given the opportunity.

He stroked a strand of hair away from my face as I licked and kissed the sweetened cream from his body. I found myself running my hands across his arm, letting him know that I felt it too. But was this all an act? Did he make every woman he was with feel this good, this wanted, this desired? Did his cock stir at any woman or was it only for me?

Once I was done, he pulled me back on to his lap, shooting a look backstage where I could see a few of the other dancers raising their eyebrows at him expectantly. Reluctantly, Chad got to his feet. He took a deep breath before he turned to the audience once more, like he was forcing himself back into the mindset to perform all over again.

Women roared their approval as he approached the front of the stage once more, guiding me along with him, his arm still tucked around me tightly as though he didn't want to let me go.

"Give it up for Madison!" he called out, and there was a huge round of applause.

I leaned against him, not wanting this to be over. I knew there had to be more to the show that just turning me on, but I didn't want there to be.

He leaned down and scooped me up off the ground, making me squeal with surprise. Instinctively, I wound my arms around his neck and clung on tight, for dear life. He made his way off the stage and back down towards my seat. People moved out of the way quickly to let him through.

I let my head rest on his strong shoulder, inhaling his scent one last time, wanting to commit as much of this to memory as I could. I wondered how obvious I was being, and swiftly decided that I didn't give a shit. If I was the kind of person who got up on stage at a male strip show, then I was the kind of person who didn't care what people thought of me when I did.

He placed me back down in front of my seat, and I was sure that was it. It had just been a seriously good play on his part, a practiced performance. A testament to how good he was at his job. But, to my surprise, he produced a small scrap of paper from somewhere I didn't want to think about and tucked it into my cleavage. His fingers just brushing across my breasts. It was enough to send shivers up my spine. He leaned in close, one last time, his mouth brushing for the briefest moment against my ear.

"Call me," he murmured.

CHAPTER 9

MADISON

With my jaw on the floor, I watch him head back on stage to join the rest of the dancers who had come out to pick up where they'd left off. I pulled the note from my chest and saw a series of numbers on it. Was this real? Was this part of the act? It felt real. He couldn't fake that kind of chemistry. Could he?

I turned to Eleanor, and as soon as I saw her face, I knew I was in trouble. Big trouble. She was seething, so much so that I was surprised steam wasn't pouring out of her ears.

"Come on," she grabbed hold of my wrist and pulled me to my feet. "We need to go to the bathroom."

I followed her, stumbling along behind her as she strode out of the theatre. I looked up at Chad and saw him watching us. Defiantly, I flashed him another dizzy smile. As soon as Eleanor and I made it into the bathrooms she turned on me at once, face dark.

"What the fuck was that about?" she snarled, waving her hand in the direction of the stage.

"What do you mean?" I grinned, the paper still clutched tight in my hands.

"You behaved like a bitch out there."

I gasp. "It was just a bit of fun. He picked me, that's all."

"What kind of friend are you? You know that I came here to get with him and you go and take him for yourself," she fumed, raising her eyebrows as though that was supposed to mean something to me.

"I didn't take him," I protested. "And I can't help that he picked me out of the crowd—"

"You could have sent me up instead," she interrupted furiously. "You knew I needed this. You didn't even want to come."

I frowned. "I'm sorry, I guess I wasn't thinking in that moment," I apologized, even though I really felt I had nothing to apologize for. But I knew Eleanor, and I knew that if I didn't concede my position to her the rest of the night was going to be a fucking nightmare.

"Yeah, I bet you weren't," she snapped. "Just like you weren't thinking when you put on that dress."

"What do you mean by that?" I ran my hands over my body. I liked the way the dress looked, doubly so now that it had gotten Chad's attention.

"You look cheap," she spat. To my horror, she suddenly plucked the piece of paper from between my fingers.

"Give it back to me," I said, as she crumpled the scrap of paper in her hands. I fought to keep the dismay from my face. It's not that I was expecting to start a relationship with Chad or anything, but I had wanted to at least see, to check if it had been his real number, and if he had actually wanted me.

"All he wants from you is a one night stand." She looked me up and down, her voice echoing cruelly through the room. It felt as if it was filling up my head making me feel quite sick. "I mean, look at you. That's what you're dressed for, isn't it?"

"El," I protested, using the pet name that she had tried to stop me from calling her a few years before. "Please, come on, it was just a bit of fun—"

"Yeah, well, I was pretty sure I was the one who was meant to be having the fun." She cocked her head at me, and then, before I could stop her, she ducked into one of the stalls, dropped the piece of paper into the toilet bowl, and flushed.

"No, Ellie, why would you do that?" I gasped as I watched my only chance at seeing Chad again spiral away into the toilet bowl.

"Because this was meant to be about me," she snapped. She walked to the door. "And I'm not going to forget that. I'm going to find him now. So you just enjoy the rest of your night."

She stormed out of the bathroom and left me standing there all alone, staring after her, wondering what in the hell had just happened and how responsible I actually was for it. I had never seen her that angry before in my life, or so I thought. And then it hit me.

All the times that she had spoken to me like this seemed to

rush up and overwhelm me all at once. There was a reason my sister hated her so much. Because this was her game, the way she'd always treated me. I always had to be less-than her, always had to be propping up her pathetic ego. And now, as the sound of the flushing toilet faded away, she had just blown my chances for a bit of fun with a hot guy because she couldn't handle the fact that he had picked me over her.

I retreated into one of the stalls and closed the door behind me. I wasn't sure how long I was in there, trying to make sense of what had just hit me like a ton of bricks. Women came into the toilets, they laughed, they talking among themselves, they used the other stalls. They even tried my door. Then they left.

I felt stupid for not guessing it sooner, but now, here I was, stuck on a night I had never wanted to come out on in the first place, and wondering why the hell I had let that kind of woman stay in my life for so long.

Eventually, the music and the cheers and the chatter faded away outside the bathroom, and I got to my feet and went out. I washed my hands and automatically checked my make-up.

She would probably already be out of here, and knowing her probably with Chad? Would he fall for her game? My heart sank at the thought, and I pushed it out of my head as I made my way out of the bathroom. I tried not to cringe at how much the taxi was going to cost back to my place now that I wasn't splitting it with anyone.

My feet were killing me. Peeling my heels off my feet, I trudged out of the bathroom, and out into the lobby. The place was empty. Everyone else had headed home, likely at the end of a good night with their friends. I could still remember how it had felt to arrive here, how it had felt to be surrounded by the buzz of excitement that hung in the air as we waited for the show to begin. That felt like so long ago now.

"Hey," called a voice from behind me.

CHAPTER 10

MADISON

I turned around tiredly, thinking it would be an usher letting me know that the place was closed and telling me to go home already. But, to my utter shock, I found myself looking at the man who had caused all the commotion in the first place.

"Oh!" I squeaked, blinking at him stupidly.

"Sorry, did I sneak up on you?" He grinned. He was fully-dressed now, in a pair of dark jeans and a form-fitting black shirt that didn't do justice to the muscles underneath that I had so recently had a front row seat to.

"Yeah, a little," I admitted. "But it's okay."

"Are you alright?" he asked, frowning.

I shook my head and lowered my gaze. I felt embarrassed that I was dragging him into this, but I knew it was written all over my face. I really was upset about everything that had happened over the course of the evening. Well, not what had gone down with him, but all that had happened with Eleanor still felt like a damn kick to my teeth.

"What happened?" He moved towards me, and placed a comforting hand on my arm. I felt that explosion of tingles once more, as soon as our bodies connected, but he was just being nice, that was it.

"My friend and I had a falling out and she left without me." I shrugged, trying to sound as though I didn't give a shit, but my voice shook. I just cared too much about everything. That was what had gotten me into this mess in the first place. If I had just been able to turn Eleanor down for this evening none of this would have happened.

"Man, that sucks." He cocked his head at me, and I looked up into those bright eyes and reminded myself that this hadn't been a complete write-off, after all. As long as I live I will never forgot what happened on stage. That one hot gorgeous man wanted by a theater full of women picked me, wanted me.

"Can I buy you a drink?" he suggested. "The bar's still open. Seems like you could use it."

"Seriously?" I raised my eyebrows at him. He must have taken my shock at him actually asking me out for a drink as some kind of reluctance, because he held his hands up at once.

"Hey, if I'm overstepping—"

"No, no, I'd love to," I assured him, and to my astonishment I found myself fluttering my eyelashes at him even though I was still cut up about everything that had just gone down with Eleanor. But somehow, that hurt seemed to drop away when I looked into his sparkling blue eyes.

A smile cracked over his face, and he held his hand out to me. "Come on, babe. I'm going to show you a good time."

CHAPTER 11

CHAD

I had never had it happen like that before, not in my life.

I had used so many women from the audiences of my shows before, so many women who anyone else might have thought of as hot, sexy, or desirable. And sure, I enjoyed the attention for as long as it lasted, but I never wanted anything more from them. But this woman?

This woman was a whole other story.

I watched her as she was dragged unceremonious by her jealous friend towards the bathroom. I knew she was about to get her ear chewed off, but all I could see was the way that dress clung to her. It was enough to get me hard again.

I had noticed her the moment I stepped out onstage, the rest of the crowd vanishing from my line of vision as my surprised eyes took her in. In that blue dress, with that cleavage, the way her hair tumbled down around her shoulders like it was waiting for me to run my hands through it.

No wonder her friend had been jealous.

The bar was quiet, much to my relief. Sometimes the women who'd attended my shows would hang around after it was done in the hopes of catching me. A lot of them threw themselves at me. It was part of the job, I got it, but sometimes it was a little exhausting to always have to be on.

But the way Madison looked at me, I knew that she felt that frisson too. She had felt the same connection that had rumbled deep inside me from the second I laid eyes on her. There was no way she could have missed it. From the moment I saw her I wanted her. Even from across the table I could still smell her perfume, something sweet and light and floral, and all I wanted was to bury my face in her neck and lose myself there for a while.

"Hey," she picked up the glass of wine she'd ordered. "So…"

"So," I grinned. I felt like the whole night was spread out in front of us, and there was so much I wanted to do with her, to her.

"Just so you know," she lowered her gaze as though she couldn't believe she was saying this. "I totally would have called you if Eleanor hadn't gotten rid of your number."

"Well, I'm only in town for one night." I shrugged. "You've gotta take those chances, right?"

"Right," she agreed, and I noticed her gaze flicker down to my mouth for a moment. I grinned. I was used to having women attracted to me, but it had been a while since I had felt that attraction burning straight back at them.

"So, what do you do in a town you're only in for one night?" she asked, cocking her head at me, and taking another sip of her wine.

"I don't know." I shrugged again. "Usually I just have a drink and get some rest. Being up there all night is pretty exhausting."

She nodded. "Oh, yeah, I can imagine. I saw the way you were moving up there. It was…uh, pretty intense." She lowered her gaze once more, as though she couldn't believe she was actually talking with me. I saw her force herself to look back up and into my eyes.

"You know I wasn't even going to come to this thing tonight?" she admitted, leaning a little closer.

I leaned in to meet her and caught the sweet scent of her perfume once more. "Oh yeah?" I grinned.

"Yeah, if it hadn't have been for my friend, or rather ex-friend, I wouldn't have met you." She bit her lip. She kept doing that, as though she was trying to keep from blurting out something she didn't intend to. I knew exactly how she felt.

"Well, I guess we have something to thank her for," I remarked, letting my hand stray onto her thigh. She inhaled sharply when I touched her. The warmth of her skin, even through the fabric of her dress, had my cock stirring in my pants once more. I could still remember the way her tongue had felt on my skin, the warmth of her breath. Fuck, it was incredible, but I wanted to just grab her by the hips and fuck her right there on stage.

Slowly, she lifted her gaze to meet mine. I had seen desire enough times to know it, and I could see it in her eyes now, what was no doubt reflected in mine. I had to do something. I was in this country for twelve more hours and I was sure as hell going to make the most of my time by spending all of it with her.

I leaned in, breathing deeply, filling my head with the scent of her, and she closed her eyes.

"Chad..." she murmured my name. I could see this tiny drop of wine on the edge of her mouth, and I finally touched my lips to hers and tasted her at last.

Her body trembled as I ran my hand up her leg and let it come to rest on her waist. I wondered how deep her desire went, if she was just testing herself to see how far she could go, or if this was really going to happen. I pulled back, and she leaned her head against mine for a moment, eyes still closed, and flicked her tongue across her full bottom lip.

"Where are you staying?" she asked, her eyes open again.

I realized I had sunk my fingers into her waist, like I was trying to leave an imprint on her. "In the rooms upstairs." I flicked my eyes upwards. I could feel the gaze of the bartender on me, the few other patrons in this bar sensed the chemistry between us. I didn't care.

"Take me there," she demanded, her lips parting slightly.

CHAPTER 12

CHAD

I needed no more encouragement. It took everything I had not to scoop her up, flip her over my shoulder, and carry her luscious curves up there like the caveman I felt like right now, but patience won the day.

She tossed back the last of her wine and I held out my hand to her. She slipped her hand into mine, glancing around at everyone we were leaving behind, and letting out this adorable little giggle that made me want to bite her lip.

We made our way up a set of stairs to the rooms that the theatre left open for the performers to take advantage of. Mine wasn't much, but it was plenty enough for us for the rest of the night. I pulled my key out of my pocket as we turned onto the carpeted corridor that led to the bed where I thought I'd be sleeping alone tonight. She squeezed my hand and fuck, there is no way to stop myself.

I swung her around, pushed her up against the door in one motion, running my hand up her thigh, over her waist, and letting it come to a stop on her face. Her breath was fast, those gorgeous tits rising and falling so quickly it was hard not to stare, but instead, I lifted my gaze to meet hers, and kissed her once more.

This time there was no messing around, no holding back, no having to remind myself over and over again that there was not just an audience watching us but my friends and manager, who would likely be shocked. Now, it was just us, our bodies pressed together as I parted her lips with my tongue and kissed her properly.

She let out the softest little moan, somewhere between satisfaction and frustration for more, as I kissed her and I realized that I was already getting hard just touching her like this. How could one person turn me on this much?

All those women out there, all of them screaming and cheering and throwing themselves at me, and not one of them had done anything for me. Yet, she could effortlessly turn me into a raging bull. She moved her hips slightly, on instinct more than anything else, and I pushed my tongue roughly into her mouth and gripped her hair in my balled fist.

I was going to make damn sure that she never forgot me.

"Take me inside," she breathed, running one hand tentatively over my back and drawing me in close. I didn't need to be told again. I unlocked the door and the two of us tumbled into the room, practically falling over each other in our desperation to finally do this. I could still remember the weight of her in my lap as she tantalizingly and knowingly pressed herself against my cock while she played the innocent volunteer.

I intended to make her pay for that ten times over.

I picked her up, winding my arms around her and kissing her hard as I walked back towards the dresser. I dropped her down on top of it. She hooked her ankles around me. Only the thin fabric of her panties was between me and having all of her. It hit me that I could have just reached down and ripped them off and fucked her raw right there and then, but I had other plans, other things I wanted to get to first.

I kissed down her neck, slowing my pace a little. She let her hand rest on my chest, feeling my heartbeat. The sweetness of her skin was everything I'd thought it would be. Her mouth had tasted of a rich, deep wine, but her neck was all her, delicate and feminine. I grazed my teeth over her throat before I moved up to nuzzle at that spot where her neck met her ears. It made her squirm frantically and drew another one of those desperate little moans from her mouth. I decided right then and there that it was going to be my goal to get her to make as much noise as I possibly could. I didn't care if she made more noise than that entire audience out there had tonight. I wanted to hear her scream. I wanted to know she was as lost to me as I already found myself lost to her.

Truth was I was drunk on her. There was this mix deep within her this blend of something good and something bad, and I couldn't wait to tap into it and see what happened when I set it loose. Or when she did.

"Mmm, you taste so fucking good," I breathed, and she shivered once more, her eyes wide as I returned to her face to kiss her again. I held her there, just for a moment, almost tender as I trailed my tongue over her bottom lip before I drew it into my mouth and bit down softly. She moaned and ran her hands over my arms, my shoulders, my chest.

I bit her again, but harder, and earned a groan of pleasure for my troubles.

I started to work my way down once more, this time not stopping at her neck. I pushed the straps of her dress down over her shoulders and off her arms. She crossed her hands, as if on instinct, over her chest, like she wasn't used to letting people look at her like this. I liked that. I kissed her again, slowly pulling her arms aside.

"You don't have to hide from me," I whispered. "You're beautiful."

Slowly, she let her arms drop down by her sides. Finally, I got a chance to look at her incredible body full-on; her tits were gorgeous, as heavy and full as ripe fruit, her nipples brown and tempting. I leaned down to take one in my mouth, flickering my tongue against it, and then I pushed up the other and sucked them both into my mouth. I sucked and bit them until they were both swollen between my lips. She raked her fingers through my hair and moaned helplessly.

When they were impossibly swollen and her moans had become whimpers, I continued on my journey downward, kissing the soft flesh of her stomach, letting my tongue trail low on her belly just the way she had done to me.

She let out a giggle, as though the same thought had occurred to her. I kept going lower and lower until I was on my knees between her legs. I looked up, and found her lips parted, breath coming quickly. I grinned. It was so hot to know she was as turned-on by this as I was.

I took her right leg in my hand and began to kiss it, starting at the ankle. I pulled off her shoe, then moved up the inside of her calf, letting my mouth linger here and there, listening to her reactions. The speed of her breathing picked up pace as I moved closer and closer to her sweet pussy. I paused at the inside of her thigh, finding that sensitive spot that made her whole body tremble with anticipation, and slowly pushing her legs apart I rolled up the hem of her dress.

CHAPTER 13

CHAD

I leaned back to look at her then, at this woman before me. I had known that from the first moment that I had laid eyes on her in that crowd that I had to taste her. I needed her pussy in my mouth, but there was no rush, and I loved nothing more than the thought of getting her to beg me for what I was already so eager to give.

She was wearing a pair of polka dot panties, somehow so innocent, and so filthy at the same time. I moved forward slowly to plant a kiss on her flesh through the fabric. She gasped, then let out a squeak when I moved on and starting kiss down the other side of her leg.

"Please," she begged.

My cock ached at her words. She had seemed nervous at the bar, but I guessed she was as intoxicated on whatever it was that was between us as I was.

"Please?" I prompted, wanting to hear more. I wanted her to tell me every single thing she wanted me to do to her tonight, because there wasn't much that I wouldn't have done to earn those little animal-like noises of pleasure that I was already addicted to.

"Don't … I mean please, do what you were just doing," she whispered, as I reached her calf and pulled off her other shoe.

"What do you mean?" I grinned at her, letting her know that I would need to hear the words come out of her mouth before I would do it.

"You know," she bit her lip.

I hooked my fingers around her panties and held them there, demanding more from her. "Tell me," I ordered her. "I want to hear you say it."

She looked down at me for a moment longer, pressing her lips together, as though no-one had ever asked her for anything so scandalous in her entire life. Is the whole world crazy? How could they not?

"I want you to…" She took a deep breath. "I want you to go down on me."

"Good girl." I nodded approvingly, and pulled her panties off her feet and tossed them aside. I pushed what was left of her dress up and over her hips, grabbed her, and pulled her towards me in one rough motion. She raked her fingers through my hair, audibly excited, belly rising and falling quickly as I pressed my mouth against her pussy for the very first time.

The noise she made was unlike anything I'd ever heard in my life, like something had shattered inside of her for good. I quickly sealed my lips around her clit, flicking my tongue against her a few times before I settled in to a long, slow, lazy pace that told her I was going to make the most of my time right here between her thighs.

I slid my hands under her ass and guided her onto my mouth, wanting to bury myself in there and never come out if I could get away with it. She tasted so sweet, like nectar, that muskiness carving a place out for itself in my memory forever. I made sure to take my time, pulling back and licking up and down her dripping slit, looking up and watching her as I did so. She responded to every little move I made with my tongue like it was an electric shock, her face contorting and creasing with every new move I tried on her.

Sometimes, with the women I'd been with before, they had this habit of trying to look all pulled-together and sexy when I was eating them out, but she had completely given herself over to the pleasure and I couldn't think of anything hotter in the world than that.

My cock was straining against my jeans as I went down on her, stroking her clit over and over again and sinking my fingers into her thick ass as I did so. She groaned loudly, the sound ringing out around the small room, and I knew she was getting close.

I centered in on her clit once more, sucking softly, moving my tongue in gentle motions up and down, up and down, and soon she began to move with me. Holding my head in place, she rocked her hips back and forth. Holding her breath, tensing her muscles, curling her toes, and then finally, finally, coming so hard against my tongue I thought her entire body was going to fall apart.

"Fuck!" she screamed.

Tipping her head back she caught my head in an iron grip with her thighs. Her clit was pulsing on my tongue, and her pussy was slick with my saliva and her juices as she found her climax. For a long, long time the waves came as she jerked against my mouth.

Then, slowly, she came back to find I was still sucking her engorged clit. She pushed my head away roughly, her cunt was too sensitized for any more at that moment. I would have happily spent the rest of the evening turning her into a quivering, coming wreck again and again, but as she leaned down to kiss me my cock was digging into my flesh. It was desperate for release as well.

"That was incredible," she panted, her face looked as though she had just returned from an intergalactic flight. "I've never … Thank you … I …"

"Anytime," I said, and kissed her again. I loved the way the taste of her mingled on our tongues. She slid her hand down my body and gripped my cock, suddenly bold. I growled into her mouth as soon as I felt her fingers up against my erection.

"Fuck me," she murmured into my mouth, and at that moment I knew I just had to have her. There was no question in my mind. I couldn't wait any longer. I wanted to play this game all night long but for now all I needed was to feel that slick, tight pussy wrapped around my massive cock. I just hoped she would be able to take all of me, or I'd have the time to break her in. Spoil her for any other man.

I pulled her from the dresser and turned her around. She whipped off her dress and shot a look at me over her shoulder, a confident smile flickering on her face as she watched me strip down. I wanted to feel my flesh against hers, every part of her, and I needed it now.

I had some condoms in my bag. I reached over to grab one. Tearing the packet open I swiftly sheathed myself.

"Oh, God. You really are Subway Chad, aren't you?" she whispered.

"And you're going to take every last inch inside you."

CHAPTER 14

CHAD

There was a mirror opposite us, and I could see her eyes shining even in the darkness of that room. I grabbed her hip and pulled her closer, and she arched her back to press herself against me.

"I want to feel you inside me. All of you. Every last inch," she breathed, closing her eyes as if she couldn't quite believe it was her saying those words. I wondered if she'd ever done anything like this before. I certainly had, but it had never felt anything close to this. I pressed myself against her slit and sinking my fingers into her hips, and pushed my way inside her for the first time.

"Oh..." she moaned, her head dropping and her fingers tightening their grasp on the counter below her as I entered her for the first time. There weren't words to describe how good she felt around my cock; warm, tight, sweet and all kinds of perfect.

"Oh, you're so big," she breathed.

"Just a bit more," I said, as I pushed another inch into her.

"Is there a lot of more?" she asked, turning to look at me.

"Just a few inches more," I said, and thrust.

"Oh, Chad," she gasped, as I buried myself all the way in.

I held still, and didn't move for a moment as I watched the two of us together in the mirror. My entire cock was buried inside her. Not many women can take all of me. I knew that image would be seared into my memory until the day I died.

"Feel good?" I asked her.

"It's feel amazing. I'm so stretched. So full. It's amazing," she gasps.

That was my signal. I began to move. I didn't hold back. I didn't have it in me to, not after all that I'd had to repress when she had been up on stage with me. She arched her back and pushed herself back against me, moving hard, her eyes open, but half-glazed as though she could barely believe that this was happening for real. I ran my hand up her bare back and wrapped her hair around my fist, tugging it back, watching the spasm of pain and pleasure that passed over her face at my rough handling.

I had to slow down, not wanting to come too quickly, but I knew I wouldn't last forever. Seeing her like this, bent over in front of me, her thick ass shuddering with every thrust into her swollen pussy, it was enough to get my balls tingling. I was so close.

I slammed deep into her and didn't move for a moment. She moaned when I slipped my hand between her legs to find her clit once more. She turned her head and stared at me in the mirror, and the look on her face told me she was desperate for more. It sent a new rush of desire through my system that almost made me feel drunk for her.

"Come for me," I growled. "Come for me, Madison, I want to feel you come…"

I didn't have the brain space to articulate what I wanted from her any more than that, but luckily for me, it seemed to be enough for her. Her thighs trembled, her lips parted, and her body seemed to slacken beneath mine as her pussy pulsed around my cock, milking me, squeezing the last drops of pleasure from my cock.

A deep groan seemed to come from far down inside her, escaping her lips as this strange strangled cry was torn out of her she climaxed once more. Seeing the look on her face, feeling her body give out around me once more was all I needed to push me over the edge.

"Fuck," I grunted, as I felt myself go over the edge. The pleasure seemed to rip through me, setting me alight, every limb turning to ash as I did my best to keep myself upright. The sensations exploded through every nerve ending in my body. I held myself inside her for a long while, before I came back down to Earth, before I slowly pulled out.

She was still gasping for air from her own intense orgasm. I looped my arm around her waist and pulled her up and onto the bed, where she let her head sink gratefully back into the pillows.

"Holy fuck," she mouthed, the words so quiet I could hardly make them out. "That was…"

"Was?" I cocked an eyebrow and slid down the bed next to her. I could already feel something building in me again, at the sight of her generously curvy body splayed out on the sheets for me like this.

"What do you mean?" she asked, suddenly flushing a little as though she was embarrassed by what we had just done. The color on her cheeks was so cute that I had to lean forward and plant a kiss on each one. She squirmed as I let my hand trace over her stomach and down between her legs once more. Oh, this night was so far from over.

CHAPTER 15

MADISON

When I woke the next morning to the thin light filtering through the window opposite the bed, it took me a moment to work out where the hell I was. And then, as he stirred next to me and turned over, the night before came back.

Even though I hadn't had more than a glass or two of wine, I felt as though most of the night was still a blur for me. It had all been...hell, it had been more than I had ever dreamed could happen to me.

The whole night had been...it had been something plucked straight out of a fantasy that I would have written off as impossible for someone like me. But, as I carefully turned I saw the man in bed next to me, and it all came flooding back. All of it. In toe curling flashes.

It had all happened.

I had come so many times that I had lost track of the what and the how and where he had fucked me. It had started on the counter, when he had buried his face between my legs and made me come with his tongue. Then he had flipped me around to take me from behind. And then, just when I thought we were done and he was going to boot me out, he laid me down in this bed and climbed on top of me once more and…mmm. Yeah. All of that stuff had happened. Him on top, me on top, me blowing him, him eating me out, making me come with his fingers, his cock, his mouth…

Never, ever in my entire life, had there been anything like the way this played out. The chemistry between us was something I had never imagined actually existed before he had pushed me up against the door and kissed me last night. Before I had tasted his tongue in my mouth I would never have believed this kind of passion was real.

I had assumed that my attraction to him sprang from the fact that I couldn't have him, and that he was just blowing off some steam with some chick he thought was cute, but this was something else entirely. It crackled in the air the whole night long as our hands hungrily explored every part of our bodies until we were both beyond exhausted and fell asleep in each other's arms.

But now that I was awake, in the bright light on the day after, and in this hotel room with a man I barely knew, I couldn't help but feel more than a little embarrassed. I had never done anything like this for a reason, and that was because I had no clue how to handle the morning after.

I looked at my dress, my underwear, my shoes, all strewn around the room, and my heart sank when I realized that I was going to have to walk home in them. Everyone would know that I'd stayed out all night.

Damn, but I couldn't stay here; he was going back to America, and I wasn't going to hang about and make a fool of myself pretending that there was a hope in hell he might stick around a little longer for someone like me.

I snuck around the room, gathering myself, and wondered if the doors downstairs were even open yet. Maybe I'd have to hang around until someone came and opened them up for me. How mortifying…

"Hey."

A voice from the bed caught me off-guard, and I turned to find Chad smiling sleepily at me. His hair was a mess but his body was as flawless as ever, even more so now that I could actually see it in the light of the sun filtering in.

I chewed on my bottom lip. He sucked on it so much last night it was feeling a little raw, but I didn't care. I would permanently be biting my lip while he was around just to keep from groaning at how damn hot he always looked. Those sculpted abs, that taut chest, his strong arms…

"Where do you think you're going?" He climbed out of bed, stood, and stretched. Oh my! I bit my lip again. Yes, he was stark naked and his enormous cock was already stirring to life, despite the fact that we couldn't have been asleep more than a few hours.

"I was headed home." I gestured towards the door, lowering my gaze, suddenly more than a little embarrassed for him to be seeing me like this. In the harsh light of day, no doubt, he would be wondering why the hell he had taken me to bed when he could have had any one of the stunning women who had been at his show the night before.

"Really?" He cocked an eyebrow, came towards me, wrapped

his powerful arms around me, and buried his face in my neck. "You got somewhere else to be, baby?"

"No," I admitted, closing my eyes and savoring the feel of him so close to me one last time. It stung, knowing that I would have to leave him soon, but I knew it would have been stupid of me to stay.

"Then why the big rush?" he asked, pressing his mouth against my shoulder and grinding against me. I could feel myself getting aroused again, and those thoughts of insecurity and worry slid out of my head like wet paint.

"I don't want to hold you up," I said. "You have to go back soon…"

"Not that soon," he replied, slipping his hand down and letting it rest on my lower belly. He skimmed his fingers over my bush and I felt another jolt of desire lance through me. And there I was thinking I'd tapped out my reserves of pure lust after all we did the night before. But it was still there, that chemistry, as rich and intense as it had been the night before.

That didn't happen often.

"Yeah, but I don't want to be waiting around for you to go," I admitted softly. It was true. When he went, I had to go back to my life, to the reality of no job and a best friend who treated me like shit, but who would probably try to find some way to slide back into my life when this was all over.

"Then don't," he suggested. "Come back with me."

"What?" I stared at him in shock.

"Come with me," he repeated.

"Yeah, right," I said with a grin, as if I appreciated his joke. I would have loved to go back with him, but there was no way in hell he would pick up some woman he'd spent one night with and whisk her all the way back across the world with him.

"I'm not kidding," he replied, and I turned to face him. I was surprised at how unselfconscious I felt, even exposed in the light like this with him. Normally I would be doing everything I could to cover myself up, but he kept his hand on my waist and held me in close.

"What the hell are you talking about?" I demanded, brushing my nose against his softly and closing my eyes, letting myself get lost in this fantasy of him for a few more moments yet.

"I mean, come back with me to America." He pulled back and looked me dead in the eyes. There wasn't a hint of mockery in them. "I'll pay. Just for a while…until we figure this thing between us out."

"I…" I stared at him for a long moment. I had no job to go back to, my best friend had proved herself to be a completely selfish bitch, and this gorgeous man with whom I'd shared the craziest night of my life had just invited me to travel across the world with him, on his dollar.

I blinked at him. No. I couldn't. I didn't know him from Adam. Could I?

I had told myself that I couldn't do this. That I couldn't go to this show, or stand up to Eleanor, or get up on stage with him, or touch him, or make love to him, but I had done all of that. And it had brought me here. Why the hell should I stop now? With a rush of nerves and excitement, I nodded.

"I'll do it," I agreed, a smile half-a-mile wide spreading over my face.

"Seriously?" His face lit up. "You'll come back with me?"

"Just for a while," I warned. "Just to see how it goes."

"Obviously." Scooping me off my feet he laid me down on the bed and slid on top of me. Instantly, my heart-rate went through the roof. Nuzzling into my neck, he continued. "Just for a while or," he repeated my words back to me.

Then began to kiss down my chest and over my stomach, and before I knew it, I was completely lost to this man once more. I wasn't sure whether I had just made an amazing decision or a bat-shit crazy one, but in the throes of ecstasy, as if from far away I heard his voice say, "Just for a while, or until you get it, that you are mine. All mine. Forever."

The End
or
Maybe NOT!
Look out for the next installment.

CHAPTER 16

"Are you really sure about this?" I asked nervously, from my perch at the edge of the massive bed. We were in the fancy-ass hotel he'd booked us into for his last night in the country. Our room probably cost more than my entire apartment did per month.

Chad stopped haphazardly throwing his things into a suitcase and looked up at me, but before he could answer my question, there was a knock on the door. He raised a finger to indicate I should wait for his reply, and went to answer it.

I pulled the edges of the fluffy bathrobe across my chest and sat up straighter. The room service waiter seemed a little flustered as he wheeled our breakfast into the room. I stared at him curiously. When he glanced in my direction I noted the twin spots of red on his cheeks, but by the time Chad handed him his tip, he had made a fast recovery and was openly flirting with him. I guess he just had that effect on women and it would seem gay men too. God, this was going to be hard to get used to.

The door closed on the waiter and Chad poured coffee into two cups. He added sugar and cream before walking towards me with them. I took the saucer from him and murmured my thanks.

"So what issue are you doubting my resolve about?" he asked, taking a sip of his coffee.

I licked my lip and looked at him from under my eyelashes. I'd been thinking non-stop about his offer to take me back to America with him. It had seemed so sweepingly romantic and obviously perfect when he had first suggested it, but with my stupid overthinking brain, I was starting to wonder if I wasn't just letting myself get caught up in the romance of it. "About me coming with you to America. I mean, it's all a bit sudden, and you hardly know me."

"Of course, I am sure I want you to come with me."

I dropped my gaze down to the steaming liquid in my cup so he wouldn't see the desperate hope that was no doubt shining there. I was still amazed by the events of the last forty-eight hours. When I had gone out with Eleanor the day before, I had never imagined this was how it was going to end.

Hell, she hadn't either. No, if you'd asked her before we'd left my apartment who was going home with a sexy male stripper that evening, she would have confidently predicted it would be her. Just because she had just gone through a break-up, she believed the universe owed her a very hot guy. As matter of fact, the very one casually drinking his coffee in front of me as though he wasn't the finest male specimen on the planet.

My heart stung a little when I thought of Eleanor, but I

pushed her image quickly to the back of my mind. I didn't want to waste any more time on her. I just fooled myself into thinking she was a friend. All the emotion was on my side. I had to assume now that we became enemies forever from the moment Chad pulled me out of the crowd and performed his lap dance all over me.

But it was worth it.

Even now I felt a flutter in my chest when I remembered it. God, the mess of emotions running through my mind as he had touched, caressed, and tasted me. I was so nervous, but if I could go back and tell myself anything the night before, it would have been to just let it happen. It was going to be a mind-blowing experience of a lifetime.

When we hooked up after the show and went to the bar for a drink I found him a far cry from the cocky asshole I'd been expecting. Who could blame me for pre-judging him? I mean, what kind of dude gets into stripping in the first place? But he was charming and surprisingly self-contained, and he used his magnetic eyes to flirt with me outrageously. I won't lie it helped salve the fresh wound of my supposed best friend chewing me out in the bathroom to know he wanted me, not her. Who would have thought, he picked me over Eleanor!

And then, of course, we had snuck off to his hotel room to have sex and oh my…

I felt the mattress depress beside me, but I didn't turn towards him. Taking my hand between his, he turned to look at me. I avoided his gaze. I wanted so much to go with him, I was afraid he was just messing with me. Maybe this was just something he did all the time. I didn't want this beautiful fantasy I had drawn myself into in these last twenty-four hours to end.

He put his finger under my chin and raised my face. My gaze collided with his. Jesus, he was gorgeous. How long would it be before his face stopped taking me by surprise? Never before had a guy who looked even half as good as him paid even the slightest crumb of attention to me before.

It was some kind of a trip.

Even if it all ended now with the words I was about to utter, I'd forever have this amazing memory of my time with Subway Chad, the most gorgeous male on earth.

"I don't know if I can do this," I whispered.

His forehead furrowed. "Why not?"

"I can't afford it," I admitted sadly, shaking my head. "I have no money, Chad, I'm unemployed, and my savings are pretty much tapped out by now…"

Something flashed in his eyes, then he leaned in and kissed me, gently brushing his lips across mine, The gesture quieted me. I closed my eyes and kissed him back. I couldn't get enough of him, not from the moment he took me to his room above the theatre.

He pulled back, brushing his nose lightly against mine and smiled at me. "Don't you know? I'm going to pay for everything." He cocked an eyebrow at me. "The flights, whatever you need when you're there, all of it."

My eyes widened. "What?"

He shrugged. "Of course. You didn't think I was going to make you pay, did you?"

The self-reliance my mother had instilled within me pushed back against the idea of someone else paying my way. Why couldn't this guy live in the same block of apartments as me so I could not only date him, but show him off to all of my family and friends? I shook my head. "I can't let you do that. How can I expect you to pay my share of the rent, and food, and bills, and—"

He laughed. "Since I own my apartment, the rent issue won't come up. I have to air-condition the apartment whether you're there or not. As for food, so much stuff in my refrigerator gets thrown out it almost criminal. So really you'd be making me feel better about my wastage."

"Even if that were true, which I know for a fact is not—obviously you'll be spending more if I'm at your place—what would I do with my time? You have to go to work and I can't work without a visa."

"Look, can we take this a step at a time? For now, we'll just call it a holiday, hmmm? It can be as long or as short as we decide." His eyes crinkled at the corners as his eyes filled with wicked amusement. "You've never been to Miami and I've never shacked up with an English girl. We can kill two birds with one stone."

My breath caught in my throat. Wow. The idea of us living together was so out there, and yet it made perfect sense. Chad felt the draw between us the same way I did, and like me, he didn't want to let it slip away.

He rested his forehead against mine and I let out a long breath. I had no idea what to do. This was all so sudden, and even the idea of following someone halfway around the

71

world was crazy. It was so unlike me. But then a little voice inside me spoke up.

"What have you got from a lifetime of playing by the rules? Where has it landed you?"

The answer was clear and brutal.

"Single, with no romantic prospects, a best friend who treated you like shit for years. While you played your part of staying nondescript so she could shine bright. You have no job and no interesting interviews lined up. Basically, your life sucks."

I frowned. Apart from my sister, Sasha, there was nothing keeping me in this country.

"Come on, be a devil," he coaxed.

Drawing back, I forced myself to look into his eyes. These bright blue eyes had picked me out from the crowd the day before. If this was some kind of crazy dream that was about to come crashing down around me all at once, I was going to make the most of it while it lasted.

I took a deep breath. "Okay, I'll go with you," I blurted out. It was completely out of character, and my agreement had to be the maddest words that had ever come out of my mouth. I couldn't believe I was agreeing to do something so freaking insane. And yet, I knew if I turned down the chance to do this, I would never stop regretting it, never stop wondering what could have happened had I been gutsy enough to go after what I really wanted. I felt as though the entire world had tilted a few inches, and everything I had been so sure about me and my future had changed.

"You'll go?" he repeated, a big happy grin breaking out over his face.

I nodded slowly. I wasn't sure I could say it again without tripping over the words, and there was no need for him to see the dorky side of me just yet.

"That's amazing." He wrapped his arms around me and kissed the strip of my neck that was exposed just above the collar of the robe. "I can't wait to show you everything. I promise you, you're going to love America..."

"I hope so," I replied nervously. My stomach was still fluttering but the choice was made. No going back on it now. Not that I wanted to.

"Now how about some breakfast?"

"I only want a slice of toast."

He grabbed my hand and pulled me to my feet.

"Come on. Eat it before it gets cold. I need to finish packing,"

"Aren't you going to have any?"

He grinned, a wicked, wolfish grin. "The only thing I'm hungry for is pussy, which I intend to have once I've fed you."

I couldn't keep a smile from cracking out over my face. This was really, actually happening. Even though it felt impossible, this man was crazy for me.

"Where in America do you live?" I asked as I buttered my toast. There was so much basic information about him that I didn't even have a grasp on.

"Miami, of course," he replied cheerfully, as though it should have been obvious. "It's the real city of sin, let me tell you."

"You can just show me," I replied, not realizing how flirtatious those words sounded until I'd said them. I flushed a little, and then remembered that I didn't have to worry about holding back, not with him. We had already hooked up and it had been incredible, and watching him move around this place in that tight black shirt and a pair of well-cut jeans must have illuminated that side of me once again. He turned to me, eyebrows raised, slowly closing his suitcase as though to indicate that he was done with packing.

"I guess I should be getting back to my place to pack," I remarked, popping the last bit of toast into my mouth.

He moved towards me, sure and confident. Slipping his arms around my waist, he pulled me against him. "But what about my breakfast?" he murmured tantalizingly into my ear. He moved lower and kissed my neck with butterfly kisses. I felt my knees begin to buckle underneath me, and I hooked my arms around his neck and hung on for dear life.

"I guess you could have some," I replied, voice already hoarse, and with that he hitched me up off the ground and carried me through to the bathroom. I hung on to him and giggled.

"What are you doing with me?" I demanded still laughing, and he set me down next to the enormous shower and leaned in to switch it on, and then pulled off his shirt.

"Setting the table for breakfast," he replied, turning me around and beginning to undo the belt of my robe. I closed my eyes and grinned as I felt his fingers on me. And I knew, in that moment, I had made the right choice.

CHAPTER 17

CHAD

Her robe fell away from her onto the floor. Underneath, she was wearing nothing but the black suspender belt and stockings that I had not allowed her to remove last night. The stark darkness against her white skin was incredibly erotic to me.

I ran my hands over the curve of her waist and down to her hips. Drawing her back against me I kissed swiftly up her shoulder and along her neck. She tilted her head to allow me all the access I wanted, and I let my fingers stray lower and sink into her ass.

Some part of me stood awed. Almost in disbelief that this woman was all mine. I knew last night had been a long shot, but I couldn't let whatever our connection was go that easily, not a chance in hell. I had travelled enough and slept with enough women to know when I shared something special with somebody, and what I shared with Madison was fucking crazy.

"Mmm," she groaned softly.

I ran my hand over her throat, kissing her slowly, letting my tongue linger on her lips before I pushed it into her mouth. My cock was already rock hard as I pulled back and nudged her towards the shower.

"I think you should get in," I said.

She walked under the rain-head shower, suspenders and all. I watched the water droplets land on her body and flow down in rivulets. So hot. Then the little minx coyly turned her back to me and executed a little shimmy, shaking that peachy ass for all it was worth. Widening her legs she pushed her butt out and made her pussy peek out between the round globes. Water coursed down her back and over her spine as though creating an arrow pointing to where I needed to be

A deep growl of desire rumbled out of my throat. I was pretty sure it made me sound like a fucking caveman, but I didn't give a crap. All I cared about was that I had my woman naked, wet, and ready to go. Without taking my eyes off her inviting pink folds, I undressed quickly. As soon as I was naked and sheathed I joined her, letting the water pour over our bodies together.

"You look so fucking good like this," I breathed, not sure if she could hear me over the sound of the running water and not caring. It wasn't like I wasn't going to tell her that a million more times anyway.

She turned around, wrapped her slippery arms around me, and kissed me deeply while pressing her entire body against mine. There was something undeniably sexy about that, about feeling her tits and her pussy against me and knowing it was all there for me. She wriggled her ass against my cock and moaned again, the noise impossibly sexy. I wanted to prolong the moment, but my dick was getting painfully insistent and I was aware I needed to do something about it.

"I need to be inside you right now," I whispered in her ear.

Obligingly, she put her hands on the tiled wall. I didn't need any further encouragement. As I grabbed her hips, she arched her back and pressed back against me. I had hooked up with a good girl, but she was turning out to be fire. There was no denying the smoldering heat in watching a good girl pull shit like this.

Fisting my erection, I pressed it against her slit. Slowly, taking my time, I eased myself inside of her and savored the feeling of her tight, wet pussy around my length. Some girls couldn't take all of me, not Madison. She took me to the hilt.

As my cock spread her open she gasped with pleasure. She half-turned her head to me so I could see the look of sheer bliss written all over her face. Her eyes were closed and mouth gaping open. Water flowed into it.

I ran one hand up her front and began to play with her nipples, pinching and toying with them until they grew hard under my hands. Would this ever get old? I usually lost interest in hooking up with someone as soon as I had done it a couple of times and sometimes as soon as I'd had them once, but Madison, I just wanted more and more. Like some kind of heroin junkie I craved her. She just felt so fucking *good*, her body, her pussy, her tits; everything seemed as though it had been made for me, to fit into my hands, against my body, to accept into her body.

I began to fuck her, going slow at first, and then picking up the pace until I was practically matching the water rushing down us. I drove into her hard so hard she began to grunt. As

I withdrew I let my hand land on her curvy ass in a sharp slap on one cheek. Her flesh jiggled and she squirmed with pleasure in response. This wasn't like last night, when I had wanted nothing more than to pleasure her all night long. No, this was just raw, unbridled desire.

I wanted to see her ass red.

I couldn't tell how long we fucked, but I was inside her for long enough to permanently burn the image of her like that into my brain. The look on her face, the noises she made that I could hear over the water, the way she pushed back eagerly to meet my thrusting cock.

After a while, I let my fingers stray forward to her clit, stroking the silky nub very gently. The contrast between the intense way I was fucking her and the tender way I was playing with her sweet clit very quickly dropped her over the edge. And how she went. Her jaw clenching, her eyes opened wide, her thighs trembling uncontrollably, and her pussy clenched like a vise around my cock.

I swear to God, I'd never seen anything sexier than the way she totally abandoned herself to her climax. I tried to hold back just so I could watch the waves crash into her, but I couldn't. Slamming hard into her as I came too. I held myself deep inside her for a few more moments, and then slowly, reluctantly, withdrew. Quickly disposing of the condom, I hooked an arm around her waist to keep her from toppling forward.

She was breathing hard and fast as she wrapped her arms around my neck. We kissed deeply then, her fingers running over my sodden scalp, and when she pulled back I could see that her cheeks were flushed. Without her makeup she was even more beautiful.

"That was amazing," she mouthed against my lips.

I let one hand rest on her generous, reddened ass, and reached for the shampoo. "It was. I guess it's time I got you cleaned up."

"Yes, I guess you should, because I have been a very dirty girl."

I laughed, and she closed her eyes and smiled, as blissful as I'd ever seen her.

Pouring out shampoo into my palm, I turned her around and began to massage her scalp using firm, circular motions letting the suds build up.

"Mmmm…"

"Yeah, you go ahead and relax, baby, because I still have to have my breakfast."

CHAPTER 18

MADISON

"Sorry, you're going to do *what?*"

I knew that telling my sister was going to be the hardest part, but I still had to pull my phone away from my ear to keep my eardrum from bursting when she reacted to the news. That hadn't been as enthusiastic as I was hoping for, if I was being totally honest with myself.

"I'm … uh, I'm going to America," I repeated, wincing and pinching the bridge of my nose. I knew my sister was the one meant to look out for me when I was doing stupid shit, and for sure this could be put under that umbrella, but I could really have done with her support. I already felt as though my brain was going to drop out the back of my head at the shock of what I was doing.

"You're serious," she said in a daze, as though trying to process what I was saying to her. "You actually mean this."

"Yeah, I do," I replied. "I know it's…I know it's a lot to take in, and I know it's super fast, but—"

"When did you meet this guy?'

I cleared my throat. "Er…last night—"

"Last night?" She stopped me before I could get any further. "What, at the strip show? I thought you were there with Eleanor?"

"Yeah, well, Eleanor and I had kind of a falling out," I explained awkwardly. "I don't think we'll be seeing each other again any time soon."

"Well, that's for the best," Sasha agreed with me on that one, at least. "But this guy? Who is he?"

"He's one of the strippers," I replied, and I couldn't help but grin when I thought about my man. "The main one, actually."

"You need to slow right the fuck down, Sis," Sasha exploded. A crinkle of static came down the line. "Because I need to get this straight. *You're* going to America with one of the *strippers?*"

Suddenly I could see how it must sound to anyone with half a brain. "Yes."

"Oh, Jesus." She took a deep breath. "How can you afford it?"

"He's paying for everything," I replied. "And putting me up in his apartment for … however long, I'm not sure yet, to be honest."

"Be straight with me," she demanded, "you've already slept with this guy, right?"

"Yeah," I admitted. There was no point trying to keep anything from my sister; she would always see straight through me.

"So, is this like, a situation where you're running away to get married?"

I shook my head, even though she couldn't see me. "No, no, it's not like that," I assured her. "It's just…"

"It's just that you're dropping everything to move halfway around the world to be with a guy you barely know. You have to know how crazy that sounds, right?"

"Well, when you put it like that…"

"How else would you put it, Madison?" I could hear the concern in her voice. She was my sister, after all, and she only wanted the best for me. I knew that. Of course, I knew that. She just didn't understand. What had happened between me and Chad was not normal. The whole thing was crazy. Right from get go.

"I know it sounds completely bonkers. And trust me, there is not a thing you can tell me that I haven't already thought of, but my life here has been such a mess recently, Sasha. What harm can it do if I just saw it as a holiday. Don't I deserve one after all I've been through. Besides, I don't want to just sit around waiting for something to happen when someone has come along and offered to actually *make* something happen for me. You know what I'm saying?"

She fell silent for a moment, and I knew she was considering what I had told her. "So how long are you going to be gone for?" There was resignation in her voice. She knew there would be no talking me out of this decision, no matter how strongly she disagreed with it.

"I don't know yet," I admitted. "But I'll let you know as soon as I do."

"And when are you leaving?" she asked.

I felt a twinge of sadness when I realized that I wouldn't have a chance to see my sister before I went, but I knew I would be back soon enough. Chad would get tired of me soon. "Tonight," I replied regretfully. "I'm actually packing right now. I just didn't want to call you from America and have you find out that way."

"Well, I appreciate the thought," she replied grimly. "You take care of yourself, alright, Madison? Don't get into any trouble. And don't be too proud to come back if things don't work out. You know I'm going to roast you for it either way."

"I know." I managed a grin. "I'm going to miss you, Sasha."

"I'll miss you too, babe." She sighed. "Good luck out there. Just remember I'm here for you. No matter what."

"Thank you."

We said our goodbyes. They went on longer than I had expected, but I guess my sister was really worried about her little sister. After that I went back to packing my stuff up. I couldn't take too much. It wasn't like I had an abundance of clothes that would be fit for Miami anyway. Most of my wardrobe was designed for the cold British weather, not glowing sunshine or the beach. Miami was near a beach, right? I would have to look that up before I went out there.

Holy hell, I still couldn't believe any of this was happening.

After I had packed a suitcase, I scanned my tiny little apartment and felt a little pang. I couldn't imagine someone else in here, not while all my stuff was still here. This was my home for the last three years. No matter how shitty the past few months had become this was my sanctuary. I couldn't believe I was really leaving this all behind.

Of course, my rent would still get paid on the 15th of the month, but if things worked out with Chad then there would be no reason for me to return. And then I caught myself. This was how hearts got broken. This was just a holiday. This was my apartment and I would be back. A message pinged on my cell.

Taxi outside.

"See you soon," I said aloud to the air in my home, as I picked up my suitcase and walked to the door. My heart was filled with excitement for the future.

The driver heaved my suitcase easily into the boot of his car and we headed out of the city. Chad and I had agreed to meet at the airport, but as I looked out of the window I remembered the doubt in Sasha's voice, the worry and concern for me, and I wondered if I wasn't making a huge mistake. What if I got my heart broken.

But then Heathrow terminal came into view, and as we cruised up to Departures, I saw him standing on the curb looking around anxiously. He was waiting for me as if there was some doubt in his mind that I might not come, and the way his face lit up as soon as he laid eyes on me made a wave of relief course through me. It might be crazy, but it was the right choice, the only one I knew I could make. Any other would have caused me to live in regret.

Before I knew what was happening he had paid the driver, transferred my luggage from the car to his trolley, drawn me into his arms, and pressed his lips to mine very quickly. "You know, I could have afforded the cab," I protested breathlessly.

"I know you could," he replied. "But this entire journey is on me. Come on, let's check in."

He led me to the airline's first class desk.

"We're flying first class," I whispered shocked.

He put his forefinger across my lips. "Money is useless if you don't spend it."

I could feel excitement coursing through my body as I stood next to him and watched him take control of all the arrangements. I noticed people, well women, giving him funny looks as though they knew him from somewhere, and it took everything I had in me not to lean forward and let them know that yes, that was Subway Chad, and yes, he really was big, and yes, he *really, really* was travelling with me.

At every opportunity he tried to make a physical connection with me, holding me so close, linking his fingers with mine, winding an arm around my waist, always making sure our bodies touched in some way. He didn't let me carry a bag either, which actually made me feel slightly strange because I wasn't used to a guy being so chivalrous to me. I had grown up opening all my own doors, but I had to admit it made me feel special. As if I was delicate and needed to be protected.

We were whisked through the fast lane passport control. I'd been flying since I was a kid, but hell, this was completely different experience than cattle class. The difference between night and day. No queuing up, no one rudely asking you take your shoes off, no one looking at you as if you were hiding an explosive in your jacket. It was an extraordinarily civilized procedure. The way it should be for everyone, not just the very rich.

When we were through security, we were whisked off away from the rest of the crowds and towards an almost empty, luxurious lounge.

"Wow," I mouthed, glancing around. The lights were muted, the carpet was dark and thick, the sofas looking wide and inviting. It was more like a private club than an airport lounge. A frosted glass enclosure promised relaxing foot massages beyond it. There was only one other couple in there. They were sipping on some kind of expensive-looking green drink.

"See why this is the only way to fly." He flashed me that playfully-cocky smile of his.

"Yeah, if you have the money," I muttered.

He leaned in to kiss me, and I felt that explosive feeling in my chest once more. I wasn't sure whether it was dangerous or benign, but I knew that it came every time I found myself close to him and there was nothing I could do to change that.

We drank champagne and whispered to each other about the prospect of joining the mile-high club. At that moment, there was no one else in the world but us in that darkened lounge, and it was beautiful. Half-tipsy, I was pulled up and led to the departure gate. To my surprise the air-steward greeted us both by name and showed us to our seats. I say seat, but really, it was a bed. Thanks to its fully reclining nature and silky duvet I was given, I passed out in the first five minutes.

I woke up to Chad gently squeezing my hand to draw me back to consciousness.

"We're almost landing," he said with a smile.

"Oh, what about the mile high club," I mumbled.

He smiled. "Next time. You sleep well?"

I nodded, yawning and covering my mouth. "Sorry, I slept off."

His smile broadened. "It was my fault for keeping you up all night."

"Hope I didn't snore."

He shrugged. "I think it bothered everybody else more than it did me."

My eyes widened in horror.

"You didn't snore, don't worry," he assured me, with a chuckle. "I just couldn't resist."

"Dick," I muttered.

Then an air hostess came up to give me a hot towel and asked if I wanted any coffee. All with a million-dollar smile. It was so unfair that everyone couldn't have this treatment.

Soon enough we were out of the plane and into a cab. On our way to his apartment. It felt as though things had gone so quickly. It was late evening in Miami, and I had my face practically pressed to the window of the car so I could take in everything passing me by.

"Like what you see?" Chad asked, reaching over to rub between my shoulder-blades.

"I really do," I said nodding vigorously. "Holy shit, is that an actual palm tree?"

"It is," he grinned as I looked up, wide-eyed, at the thing towering over us. "You've never seen one before?"

"Not in person," I shook my head and leaned back in the seat. "Holy fuck, I can't believe I'm actually here."

"Let's take it slow," he suggested. "Don't want you to get overwhelmed."

"I think that's pretty much inevitable," I murmured, mostly to myself; I already felt as though my brain might come leaking out the back of my head at any given moment, this was all so much to take in all at once.

"You want to get something to eat? I could use a meal."

I nodded, unable to tear my gaze away from everything that was in front of me. We were coming into the city, and all I could see was neon and bright lights for miles. We passed little clusters of people out on the town, dressed in scraps of clothing so tiny they made me cringe a little. Perhaps people like me were best suited to living in colder countries where we could hide in layers of clothing. Outfits like these would have got one frozen to death in England.

Into my vision came a gaggle of women dressed to the nines in heels and dresses. they looked amazing. I looked down at my outfit, a set of jeans and a shirt. "I think I need to get changed first,"

"How about we stop by the apartment, freshen up, and then head out?" he suggested.

"That sounds good," I replied, and turned my attention back

out the window once more. I was still reeling, my brain trying to wrap itself around the fact that I'd been drinking coffee with Eleanor barely a couple of days before, and now here I was on the other side of the world with a man by my side who couldn't seem to get enough of me.

It didn't make any sense, but I loved every second.

CHAPTER 19

MADISON

When we arrived back at his apartment, he went to switch on the air-conditioning and I looked around me curiously. It was way bigger than my place and very neat. It didn't even look like anyone lived there. All the leather sofas looked immaculate and new and the glass tops shone brightly.

He came back. "Come on, let's change and get out of here. I'll show you how everything works when we get back."

The bedroom was four times the size of mine back home. It had a massive picture window that looked out over the beach. I walked to it and looked out.

"Wow, you have beach front property."

"Yup."

"It's gorgeous, Chad." I turned to look at him. "You're so lucky."

He looked deep into my eyes. "I am lucky. Very lucky."

"Maybe I'll take a walk down on the golden sands tomorrow, enjoy the cooling water a little."

"Or maybe you'll spend the whole day in bed with me."

I shook my head, still quite unable to believe that he wanted me that much.

"Go on and change, or I'll be having pussy for dinner."

He slapped my ass as I scuttled away from him. I emerged after a few minutes, after pulling on the same blue dress that he'd seen me in the night before. I was a bit embarrassed to be getting into the same dress again, but I didn't have a huge range of clothes to choose from that would suit a formal restaurant setting. None of that mattered when he turned around and saw me. His eyebrows shot up.

"You're determined to make me suffer, aren't you?" he observed, moving towards me. He ran his hands down my waist, tracing the curve that led into my hips, and I closed my eyes and thought about calling off dinner right there and then. To my horror my stomach grumbled and he laughed. "Right. Food for you. You need something to eat if you're going to have the energy to do everything I want you to do later tonight." He lowered his voice. "Yes, that's right. I'm not stopping until you beg for mercy."

"Or you beg for mercy," I shot back.

He laughed. "Promises, promises."

"So, do you have a place in mind for dinner?" I asked shyly as I hooked my arm through his and he led us to the door.

He shrugged. "There are couple of places I've been missing since I've been on tour," he replied with a smile. He seemed so at-ease in this place, and his comfort helped bring me back down to Earth.

"Oh, yeah?"

"Yeah, there's this awesome pizza joint a few streets over," he said excitedly. "Really upmarket. And the food is fucking incredible."

"That sounds perfect." Now that he had said the word 'pizza' I couldn't think of anything that I wanted more in the world.

He took me to his car, which was parked in a garage attached to the apartment. It wasn't flashy, but it suited him. A classic convertible in sky-blue, with deep wood detailing.

"My pride and joy," he said with a grin. "I got her with the very first paycheck I ever had for my stripping, and she's been with me ever since."

"When did you start with all of that?" I asked, curious. I knew so little about him, and I guessed this would count as our first date, of sorts, even though it was coming after I'd moved halfway around the world to be with him.

"The stripping?" He raised his eyebrows, as though casting his mind back. "Damn, it's been such a long time...probably about nine years?"

"Nine years?" I exclaimed. "I don't think I've done anything for that long in my life."

"Well, trust me, when you find something you love and that you're good at, it's not hard to stick it out," he replied. "That was actually my second tour around the world. I love travel-ing. Sometimes I wish I didn't have to do the shows every evening, though, since it cuts into how much of the nightlife of wherever I am I can enjoy."

I ran my hands over the smooth walnut wood on the dashboard as he climbed in next to me. He kept the top down, but the air was warm enough so I didn't even mind.

"You're a nightlife kind of guy?" I snuck a look at him out of the corner of my eye as he pulled out and onto the street.

Reaching over he squeezed my leg. "I'll show you just what kind of guy I am later."

We made it the rest of the way in silence, both of our minds taken up with everything we were going to do as soon as we finished dinner and got back to his apartment.

He came around to open the car door for me like the gentleman he was, and offered me his arm. I slipped mine through the crook of his elbow and we headed into the restaurant. The place was packed and I was sure that we weren't going to get a table, but as soon as the host lifted her eyes and laid eyes on him, a big-ass grin broke out across her face. She stepped away from her stand and waved her arm over the restaurant.

"How nice to see you again, Chad?"

"Same here, Lily."

"For two?"

"For two, and Lily, give me the best seat, won't ya."

Lily turned her gaze to me, even though I had been standing right there on his arm the whole time I had been invisible to her, but Chad asking for the best table had somehow put me back on her radar. I saw a little bit of the sparkle drop out of her gaze. I ignored it. She was probably just disappointed that she wouldn't be able to flirt more tips out of Chad, given that I was here. Nothing to take to heart, but I knew it was nothing to do with tips.

She led us over to a table next to the window, with a view down over the beach that made my heart sing. I stared out across the waves, softly lapping up the golden beach, and shook my head. "I can't believe we're actually here," I murmured, mostly to myself.

"You don't really do beaches back home?" he asked, as a waiter arrived with menus for the two of us.

"Not unless you want to spend a whole afternoon getting frostbite and wind-blasted."

He laughed, an easy, comfortable laugh, the kind that sent shivers down my spine.

"So, what's good here?" I asked, lowering my gaze to the menu and starting to flip through. I tried not to balk at the prices. He said he wanted to treat me to everything, but this was going to require some mental gymnastics for me. I was so used to being completely independent. Living off someone else was going to take some getting used.

"Pretty much everything," he replied. "But I would recommend—"

"Excuse us," A voice came from beside us, and we both looked up. I expected to see the waiter, back with the wine menu, but instead I was faced with a group of tanned, good-looking, young women. They were all staring at my date, looking hungrier than I was at that moment. I glanced over at Chad, and he seemed completely unbothered by what was happening. The girl who had spoken, the one who seemed to be the nominated head of these group, thrust a napkin and a pen at him.

"We saw your show a few months ago," she gushed, tossing her mane of perfectly-bleached blonde hair back and over her brown shoulder. "Can we get your autograph?"

Chad didn't blink an eyelid. "Sure." Quickly, he scribbled on her napkin and pushed it back in her direction. He seemed vaguely annoyed, but they weren't picking up on it.

"Thank you *so* much." She reached over and squeezed his hand.

My eyebrows shot up high enough to vanish into my hairline. Okay, what the fuck? Was this just a cultural difference that I was going to have to get used to, or was she hitting on my man right the fuck in front of me?

"No problem," Chad replied with a fixed smile. "Now, if you don't mind, I'm here with my date…"

"Oh, sorry. We just wanted your autograph."

"I understand, but I'm having dinner."

The woman gave me a dirty look before she tossed her hair and shamelessly strutted off to her table, followed by her followers who also all gave me a dirty look that was enough to curdle milk.

"I didn't realize you were that big of a celebrity," I remarked lightly.

He shook his head. "I'm sorry about that," He waved a hand in their direction. "I think they think it's cute to come up and try to hit on me when I'm out. Sometimes I think they put each other up to it."

"So this happens a lot?" I asked, already exhausted at the thought of dealing with this kind of situation.

"Yeah, it does," he admitted, pulling a face.

I could feel my heart drop. I couldn't help being jealous. I was with a man that other women were masturbating to. Ugh, no!

He leaned over and took my hand, squeezing it tight, and looking deep into my eyes. "But I'm here with you. Only you. And no-one else, alright?"

"Alright," I whispered, forcing a smile. This was my first night in Miami and I'd die before I ruined it with my jealousy. "Now, I was pretty sure you were going to recommend something for me to eat?"

We spent the rest of the evening at the restaurant talking and trying to get to know each other, but it felt like the night never really got going. Every time we would lean in, utterly involved in a conversation, or I would find myself drawn to something he was saying, something he was revealing about himself, someone else would turn up at the table to flirt, or ask for an autograph.

And it was always a damn woman.

A perfectly-maintained one who made me feel like crap in comparison, and you know what else, they never seemed to even notice I was there. By the end of the night, despite how good the food had been and how much I'd enjoyed playing footsie with him beneath the table even while those women were jacking our fun night out, I couldn't help but feel as though this was a rude awakening. A reminder that no matter how much I wanted things to be easy and smooth between us, that there were always going to be his fame in our way.

I was a bit reflective on the drive home, but I didn't think he would actually notice, or do anything about it. I'd dated plenty of guys in my time, and most of them had seen me falling silent as nothing more than a chance to go off and play video games without fear of reprisal. But Chad had a frown on his face as we walked through the door to his apartment. He stopped dead and pulled me around to face him.

"What's wrong?" he asked.

I shook my head. "No, it's nothing. Just jet lag. I think I just need a little sleep…"

"Madison, my entire career is built around knowing what women want. You can't hide that shit from me. Come on, be honest, talk to me."

He sat me down on the leather couch beside him. I sighed deeply. I had drunk two glasses of wine and really I didn't need this. All I wanted to do was go to bed with him and leave this all till tomorrow. But if we were going to do this, to *really* do this, then I supposed I owed it to him to be honest as much and as far as I could. I took a seat next to him, and began.

CHAPTER 20

CHAD

I couldn't say that it surprised me to hear her say that she was feeling down after our night out together because of all those women who thought it was okay to interrupt my privacy because they had seen me in a magazine, but it upset me to see how badly it had affected her. I laced my fingers through hers as she spoke, letting her know that I was there for her and that nothing any of those women could say or do was going to change that.

"I just wasn't ready for this level of...*anything*." She shook her head. "I know it may sound crazy to you, but I just wanted to come out here and have you all to myself."

"You do have me all to yourself," I promised. "I mean, you will. Not tonight, maybe, but as soon as..." I trailed off. Even I wasn't sure what I was getting at. I had no idea when or if ever the interest in me would drop away. It had become clear over the years I'd lived here, that when you were inextricably tied to a woman's first real chance to blow off steam and get hot for a stranger, they didn't want to forget it. I had been jousting off the interests of women around this town for as long as I'd been dancing. Sometimes, especially in the beginning, it had been fun and I had indulged them, but now that Madison was here with me and she clearly fucking hated the attention, I felt torn.

"As soon as…?" she prompted.

I shook my head and looked down at our hands, linked. I had to remind myself once more than I had only known this woman a matter of days. The connection between us was so intense that it felt as though I'd known her for years, as though my whole life was just waiting for her to appear. "I can't tell you that it's never going to happen again," I admitted. "I wish I could, but I can't."

"It's okay. I don't expect you to make any big changes for me," she said, but her face dropped, and she pulled her knees up under herself, as though trying to make herself small. I touched my other hand to her chin, tilting her face up to look at me.

"All those women tonight, I didn't even see them. They were just a blur. I didn't give a shit about any of them. Not when I had you sitting across the table from me."

She met my gaze, and I could see something lift inside her.

"I just want a chance to get to know you," she murmured. "I feel like we can't do that if you're constantly fighting off other women."

"Then we'll get takeouts, and stay in, and really get to know each other for the next week," I assured her. "Anything you want. I'm here with you, Madison, I don't want you to forget that…"

I leaned in and kissed her, and I felt her body relax as our mouths met, as though this was what she'd been waiting for.

"You mean it?" She pulled back and looked at me intently. "Takeaway, then sit in the house, and just talk?"

"Whatever you want," I replied, kissing her again.

"I don't want to stop you from doing the things you love."

"You aren't. Nothing is more exciting than being with you."

She looked up at me, her beautiful eyes clouded with doubt.

"None of those women tonight mean anything to me other than an irritation, Madison." I shook my head in wonder. "Do you really think I get off on interrupting whatever I am doing to constantly autograph the napkins of random women who I will never see again for the rest of my life?"

She exhaled the breath she was holding and smiled weakly. I felt the stiffness in her body begin to unwind, and pulled her up and onto my lap in one swift motion. I wrapped my arms around her and pulled her close. A part of me knew a moment of fear. That I wouldn't make her understand and she would get away from me. "Listen, you're the best thing that's happened to me, and I'm lucky to have you."

"God, what is it about you. I can't ever resist you," she moaned against my lips and I knew, without a doubt, that I was never letting her go, no matter what.

Her breasts were pressed against my chest and I felt her nipples harden. My cock stirred at once, pressing into her. Her reaction was to move back and spread her legs, strad-dling me. I could feel how soaked the thin fabric of her panties already was. It made me wonder how long she'd been wanting this. Maybe, if I was lucky she had craved it as deeply as I had been…

All fucking night.

She deepened the kiss, pushing her tongue into my mouth. I growled moving my hands all over her. She felt so damn *good*. That was what I couldn't get over. Every inch of her pleased me, satisfied me, did something to me that I couldn't describe; every part of her tasted good, felt good, got stuck in my memory like a record on repeat. I couldn't figure out what it was about her that did this to me, but I was sure as hell committed to finding out.

I pushed her back on the couch, climbing on top of her and moving my hand between her legs. She widened them on instinct, and I cupped my palm around the warmth of her pussy. She threw her head back with a gasp and I kissed along her neck, running my tongue over her throat, baring my teeth like an animal. Seeing her in this dress was doing things to me, reminding me of that first night when I'd seen her in the crowd and wanted to get my hands all over her and didn't know if she would allow me to. That didn't matter now. Nothing did. I just wanted to remind myself that she had given herself to me in every way I could possibly dream of.

I hooked my fingers around her panties and ripped them off her.

"I'll replace them," I promised, tossing the tattered remains on the floor. Although, I preferred to think of her living her life without panties. Naked underneath her clothes and always ready to take me into my body. I rolled up the hem of her dress and slipped between her legs. She ran her fingers through my hair and wriggled her hips encouragingly.

I kissed along the inside of her thigh. I wanted to make her wait, drive her crazy, but fuck if I wasn't starving for her taste. I pushed her legs as far apart as they would go, and looked at her pussy. There it lay between her thighs like a ripe peach, glistening with the sweet nectar of her arousal. Leaning forward with a low groan of need, I pressed my mouth against her…and felt as though I had come home.

I stroked my tongue over her slit a few times, going really slow, letting both of us get used to the feel of me feeding on her again. The taste of her, so sweet and musky, and so specifically Madison filled my mouth and spread over my tongue. I couldn't get anything close enough to it. Her fists balled in my hair, desperate and grasping, and I glanced up to see her eyes closed and her face contorted with pleasure.

Well, that was exactly how I liked to see her.

I focused my attentions in on her clit, lapping, sucking, nipping, until she was squirming like a little worm. When she was almost out of her mind with sensation, I slowed my roll and traced lazy shapes across her entire pussy, my tongue dancing around the folds as I tasted every part of her. She was rocking her hips back to meet me. Knowing how much this was getting her off was getting me seriously hard.

I ate her pussy as though it was dessert. Finally, her thighs clamped around my ears and her body began trembling. I knew that she was desperate to come, and I wanted to give her that, I really did, but not as much as I wanted to drag out her torment a little longer and enjoy the way that she shivered and shuddered at my every touch.

I slipped my hands beneath her dress and moved upwards to play with her breasts. I pinched her nipples roughly, making her moan.

"Oh, God…" she groaned, and I knew she was lost.

I sealed my lips around her clit and sucked gently while she came. So violently, I could feel her pussy pulsing like something alive beneath me. Suddenly she wrenched my head back. She had become too sensitive for more. I raised my gaze and watched as she writhed and rocked back and forth on the couch when the pleasure overtook her.

This was a memory I was going to come back to.

Making her come like this was something I couldn't imagine getting tired of, watching the way her body reacted to my touch; I rested my hands on her spread thighs, and she reached down to grab me and pull me back up on top of her. She kissed me hard, as though desperate to taste herself on my lips – the thought of that was enough to push me to a new level of desire for her, and when she pulled back, I took the opportunity to grab a condom out of the drawer on the coffee table next to us.

"Please tell me you have those in every room of the house," she panted, teasing, and I shrugged.

"Always be prepared, right?" I grinned at her, pulling down my pants and quickly slipping on the condom before I slid down on top of her once more. She drew me close, hooking her legs around me, and I took my cock in my hand and guided it into her pussy.

We both let out a sigh of what felt like relief as soon as I was inside of her. I didn't realize how much tension I had stored up inside of me waiting for this moment. She moved her hands to my face and drew me down towards her, pulling me down hungrily towards her lips as I began to move inside her.

I would never have said I had made love before in my life, not before that moment. I had fucked plenty, sure, I had screwed women and taken them and all of that. But I had never shared a moment this tender with someone prior to this, never felt this swelling in my chest of fierce protectiveness and possessiveness or this kind of connection pulse between us. Steady and regular like a heartbeat. She laid her hand on my chest as we kissed, and the sweet warmth of it even through my shirt sent shivers across my body. I thrust into her, hard, my body aching with something I couldn't put my finger on. And I watched her face reflect perfectly everything I was feeling.

I wanted to tell her none of those other women mattered. Not the ones I had been with before her, or the ones who had wanted to be with me. All that mattered was her. Was us. Here. This moment. I felt my balls tingle as I grew close to the edge. At that moment she hooked her ankles behind my back and pulled me deep into her.

And just like that, buried up to the hilt inside of her, I came.

I strained with the effort of not letting my body slump against hers as the pleasure rocked through my system. To my stunned surprise, I felt her pussy clench again around my cock, and gooseflesh appear all over her arms as she went over the edge again. I held myself inside her, not wanting to break that profound moment quite yet. Just watching her tense body relax until she seemed to almost melt into the couch below her. Reluctantly I pulled myself out of her and crashed down on the couch beside her.

"That was amazing," she whispered, getting on her side and resting her head on my shoulder.

It had been more than that. I felt as though she had launched an earthquake deep inside me, and the tremors were still shaking out over my brain and body. It wasn't just physical. No, there was something else entirely going on between the two of us, and it was more intense than anything I'd shared with anyone else before in my life.

"I guess I should get you to bed," I replied, getting to my feet, dropping a kiss on her head, and going to get rid of the condom.

When I returned her eyes were closed. She opened one. "Can't I just sleep here?" she said playfully.

I reached down and scooped her into my arms. She nestled her head against my chest. "Nope, I want to wake up next to you tomorrow."

"Can't wait for that," she said with a yawn, but she was so tired she was already asleep by the time I laid her on the bed.

CHAPTER 21

MADISON

When I woke up the next morning, for a split second, I forgot where I was. The light filtering through the enormous window opposite the bed seemed impossibly bright, and the sound of the waves on the beach below me felt like it should be a remnant from a dream.

Then it all came back.

I remembered I was in Miami with the most gorgeous guy in the world. He said he'd wanted to wake up next to me, so I reached out for his side of the bed. And found it empty. I sat bolt upright, a strange panic lancing through my system. He hadn't left me behind already, had he?

Then I heard a sound in the corridor and turned my head. Chad emerged through the door and stepped into the room. He was smiling like an angel and carrying two steaming mugs of coffees. I beamed back. I couldn't believe this was actually happening. The exhaustion from the past two days was gone and I was filled with new energy.

"Good morning," we both said in unison.

"Oh, you timed this well," I remarked, as he handed me the coffee and sat next to me. Leaning forward he pressed a kiss to my temple in an unfathomable way that felt like a habit we had shared for years.

"You were so tired, I didn't want to disturb you," he replied, taking a sip of his drink.

I did the same. It was the perfect temperature.

"So," he said slowly, watching me.

I ran my fingers self-consciously through my hair as I realized it was the first time he'd seen me so disheveled in the unforgiving morning light. I had not even taken my make-up off last night. I could only hope I didn't look too rough. Well, if I did, he was as much to blame for it as I was. It was his fault for giving me such intense climaxes. That last one had made my toes curl.

"So," I echoed.

"You're here, in Miami," he gestured around.

"Yeah, I am," I replied. "I still can't believe it."

"Me neither," he grinned, and there was just a hint of nervousness about his smile that was somehow the most endearing thing I'd ever seen. I'd dated my fair share of cocky assholes who acted as though nothing got to them, and it was nice to be around a guy who didn't seem shit-scared of his emotions for a change.

"What do you want to do now that you're here?" he asked, turning to look out across the sun-soaked beach just a few dozen feet away from us.

I looked past him to the beach beyond. "I was going to head down there and catch some rays while I have the chance, though I would need to slather myself in suntan lotion to make sure I don't end up looking like a lobster."

"And after that?"

I whirled around and stared at him curiously. "What do you mean?"

"I don't want you sitting around on your ass waiting for me all the time."

"I could walk around the town."

He nodded, but it was distractedly. He obviously had something else on his mind. "Yeah, of course, but I meant, like long-term, you know."

I frowned. "What you mean."

"Okay. Is there anything you've always wanted to do or would have loved to do, but you couldn't because of circumstances or having to put food on the table."

"I…" I trailed off and cast my mind around. It had been a long time since I actually even thought about what I actually wanted to do with my life. My dreams and desires had long-since been lost to the grind of having to make rent and as he said, put food on the table. But now that I thought about it, it jumped into my mind. I looked into his eyes and he was patiently waiting for my answer.

"I don't know, I guess I always really liked photography," I said, flushing a little. I wasn't sure why I was embarrassed about telling him, but being honest about everything that I actually wanted was still pretty new for me, and I was just getting my head around how it felt. I wasn't sure it would ever feel normal for me, but I knew it's what he wanted so I would try my hardest.

"Oh, yeah?" He had perked up, his head cocked with interest.

"Yeah, back when I was in high school I did this photography course and I fell in love with the idea of capturing the soul of something or a fleeting emotion or moment on paper," I sighed. "And then at university I was part of the photography society, but after I left, I guess I just...had to find a job that paid the bills. I never really went back to it. But yeah, if I could do anything, I would love to just take pictures all the time."

"Then that's what you will do. You will become a professional photographer," he declared confidently.

I spluttered with laughter.

"Why are you laughing? I'm serious."

"It's really flattering that you have such belief in me, but it's not that easy, Chad."

"Why not?"

"Well to start with, I haven't had any real training," I explained. "Besides, I don't have any equipment. I've looked at the really good cameras and the lighting set-ups and they cost like thousands of dollars. It's completely out of my price range."

"What about mine?" he threw back, that smile still on his face.

I stared at him in astonishment.

"I believe great photography is not about taking a course. It's about what's inside you. Photographers are born. They see things others don't, and then they take a picture of it, and show it to the world through their eyes."

I nodded, surprised by his sensitivity. Who would have thought a stripper could be so deep? "That's a very beautiful way of putting it. You're right. Photography is having the eye to see something other's don't, but there's no way I can let you pay for all of that," I protested. "It's too much. You barely know me."

"I knew you well enough to bring you into my life. Don't think this is something I do all the time. As matter of fact, I've never done this." He stroked a rebellious strand of hair back from my face. "I just don't want you sitting around here with nothing to do, wondering why the fuck you came in the first place."

"I know why I came," I replied softly, smiling at him.

"I get that," he assured. "But just...keep it mind, alright? I want you to be happy and fulfilled. I want us to have a long term plan in place."

"I'll think about it," I promised him, but I wasn't sure how I could ever bring myself to break into this conversation again.

"Good." He cocked his head at me with a grin. "I think we should go for a walk, get some fresh air, before you seduce me into bed again."

I smacked his shoulder. "Excuse me. Who seduced who?"

He looked affronted. "What? The way you looked at me that night. How was I supposed to resist that?" He looked at me slyly. "Weren't you one of the girls who raised her hand to come up."

I cleared my throat. This conversation was going down the wrong path. *Change the topic, Madison, and quickly.* "You know, I've never been much of an outdoor person, but maybe that's just because I didn't have a beach sitting at the end of my house before."

"Maybe," he agreed, leaning over to kiss me once more.

I worried about my coffee breath, but he obviously didn't give a crap about it. "Maybe I'm feeling a little more indoorsy now, too," he murmured, and flicked his gaze up to meet mine. I knew at once what was going through his mind. I put my coffee down, pulled the covers back, and invited him into the bed to join me.

CHAPTER 22

MADISON

When we were done, the sun had fully risen and the light was a fierce gold outside the window. The way it never is in England. Boy, I wanted to get outside.

"Time to go out," I warned him as I leapt out of bed, and took off.

"Mmm…" Chad lifted his head from the pillow, apparently rendered mute by everything I'd just done to him.

"You coming?" I asked, shooting a look over my shoulder as I headed into the bathroom. Once in there I was distracted by the sheer size of the place. I think the thing I would take back with me when I returned to England was how big everything in America was. The shower was a walk-in, like back at the hotel, and there was a huge jacuzzi-style tub sitting at the other end of the room. I knew Chad was loaded, but just how much money did he bring in from the dancing to be able to afford to live like this?

"I've already showered. I'm going to get dressed and make

some calls," he called back. "Come out when you're ready, alright?"

"Sounds perfect," I dithered between the shower and the bath for a moment before I settled for the shower. Something quick. I wanted to take in as much of Miami as I could, before...

As the water ran over my body, and I noticed the finger-marks where Chad had been gripping on to my hips, and wondered why my thoughts always returned to "before".

Before this perfect fantasy blew up in my face?

Before he got tired of me and sent me home?

I sighed. I knew I was treating this as though there was a due date attached, and I wasn't sure I liked that feeling. But what was I meant to do? Just bury my head in the sand and act like this guy I'd known for a matter of days was the love of my life? No matter what my heart might have been telling me, my head was still very much in play, and I wasn't going to let my heart get caught up in the fairytale aspect of all of this so quickly and with so little resistance.

I got out and stared at myself in the mirror. My skin was glowing, although, that could have been an effect of the semen facial he gave me last night. I grinned at the memory, and in the mirror, I saw a naughty look slip into my eyes. I had never seen that mischievous glint before. I must be happy.

I dried my hair, applied a little lipstick, and headed out of the bathroom to find some clothes. I heard an appreciative groan from behind me, and turned to find Chad, freshly dressed in a simple t-shirt and jeans, eyeing me up as if he was going to grab me and take me back to bed.

"Hey, you said you were going to take me out," I protested playfully, and he raised his eyes skyward for a moment as though cursing his offer.

"I did, didn't I?" He shook his head. "Come on then, get dressed, before I change my mind."

"Fine," I giggled, pulling out a light dress that hit just below the knee. It allowed for the air to circulate and I wouldn't get too warm. I was already starting to sweat lightly, despite the liberal antiperspirant I'd applied.

"You ready?" he asked. "You look great."

"Ready as I'll ever be," I nodded.

He proffered me his arm in a gallant gesture.

"Are you doing that because I'm English?" I teased.

"I'm doing that because you make me want to carry you off on a horse."

"Well, you make a good knight," I said primly, as I took his hand.

He took me to this little breakfast place, an old-school diner that did waffles and pancakes, and coffee from a bored-looking waitress with a pot who came around the booths offering it. It was perfect. Exactly, how I had imagined America to be.

"Now, this place I could live in." I leaned across the table and grinned at him.

He cocked an eyebrow. "Oh yeah?"

"Oh, yeah." I nodded, licking a drop of syrup from my fork before I took another bite of the massive waffle I had ordered.

"I'm glad you approve." He grinned, tucking into his bacon and eggs.

We spent the rest of breakfast chatting lightly about nothing serious. How long he'd lived here, where he'd stayed before. He was from a small town across the state originally, and had always wanted to move down to the coast where he knew the nightlife would be way more buzzing.

"And you always wanted to be a…?" I gestured towards him with my fork, not sure if I was allowed to say the word out in public like that.

"A stripper?" he filled in the blank for me. "No. I really did it to piss off my parents."

My eyebrows shot up into my hairline.

He grinned. "They wanted to send me off to college like my brother but I didn't want to go. So, they told me that if I could find a job that brought in the same amount he was making, then they would let me off the hook. And this was the first thing that came up."

"Holy shit." I shook my head in amazement. "That's wild."

"Yeah, well, you know me." He smiled back. "I tend to make pretty impulsive decisions."

"And you've been doing it ever since?"

"Sure have." He took a sip of his orange juice. "They came around to it eventually, but I don't think my brother ever got over the shock of knowing that I was making more than him."

"I'd like to meet him," I blurted out, then bit my lip and lowered my mortified gaze to my coffee. I couldn't believe I went there. I asked to his meet his family!

Chad laughed and squeezed my hand across the table. "I feel as if showing you off to him would be tantamount to salting the wound."

I felt a shiver of cool excitement run over my skin, so different from the intense heat of the beach.

After breakfast, we strolled hand-in-hand down the beach, but not in the direction of his apartment. I wasn't sure where we were going, but I knew that he wouldn't take me anywhere I didn't want to be. Besides I was on the most exciting adventure. I was open to all kinds of new experiences.

"You going to give me a clue where we're going?" I prompted when we'd been walking about ten minutes.

He just shook his head and tapped the side of his nose. "Patience, little one. All will be revealed in time."

Eventually, he came to a halt in front of a tech shop. When he tried to go in, I held back. "Why are we going in there? Do you need a new phone or something?"

"No," he shook his head, and tugging my hand, led me inside. "This is for you."

"What?" I followed him, brow furrowed as I tried to make sense of his words, but as soon as we stepped through the door, I found myself face-to-face with a huge, expensive digital camera, and my jaw dropped.

"You don't have to do this for me," I turned to him hurriedly. "Really, Chad, I—"

"Babe, you're wasting your breath. I've already made up my mind," he said calmly. "You Madison, me impulsive, remember?"

"But I can't let you spend this kind of money on me. It feels wrong," I protested.

"Call it a loan, then. When you're rich and famous you can pay me back with interest."

"There's no way that I'm going to be able to talk you out of this, is there?" I sighed, a little flutter of excitement in my chest as the salesman approached.

"Nope, so get on board."

In a daze I watched him drop upwards of four thousand dollars on camera equipment for me. I tried to keep my face organized so the shock wasn't too obviously, but it was hard. The most a boyfriend ever got me before this was a bottle of wine, and even then, it was usually an offer and not the color I liked.

This was insane.

The amount of cash he was spending on me was ridiculous, but by the time he finished, I had it all. The high octane camera, the memory cards, the guides, the lighting, the software to edit my photographs. Everything that I could possibly have wanted, to get started in photography, I had right there in front of me. My heart swelled with excitement as he paid. I was grateful for the opportunity, but more than that I was stunned that he thought I was deserving of all this trust.

"Thank you," I said, looking intently into his eyes as soon as we were out of the store. "I know words are nothing, but... thank you. I will pay you back. Every last cent. I promise. I can't even tell you what this means to me."

"I just want you to be able to do something you love while you're here," he replied simply, and I felt tears prick the backs of my eyes. I blinked hard so I didn't start bawling my eyes out in public. It wasn't the amount of money he'd dropped on me. No, it was the fact that he believed in me so completely, so utterly, and was so invested in me being happy that he'd thought nothing of throwing away a few thousand dollars to make that happen.

"I love having sex with you," I replied, suddenly amorous.

"So, all I have to do is buy you camera equipment to get you in the mood?" he murmured, eyes tracing the shape of my body through my dress. "Totally worth it."

"Come on, let's get back to your place," I whispered.

"Message received," he muttered, his eyes suddenly dark with passion.

The two of us sped down the beach and back to his apartment to make love for the second time that day. It felt wildly decadent, having him fuck me on the bed in the middle of the afternoon when all the sane people were at work, and in the middle of the grind.

I looked out over the beach as I lay my head down on his chest afterwards, listening to the in and out of his breath and matching it up to the waves of the sea as they crept over the golden sand and retreated again.

"I have a show tonight," he announced.

I lifted my head. "Oh yeah?"

"Yeah, it's like a back-in-town performance." He sighed as the two of us naturally sat up. He touched my face, skimming his thumb over my lips and pulling a face. "Trust me, I'd rather be here with you any day of the week, but I can't get out of this one. It's sold out."

"Right," I nodded, looking down at my hands and trying not to show just how disappointed I was. I wanted to go out with Chad tonight, take in the sparkly excess that this town had to offer, but I supposed he was going to have to go back to work sometime. The lifestyle he lived, the one that he had been showing me couldn't be sustained on great sex alone.

"But you should come along," he suggested. "Could be fun. I could get you backstage and we could fuck all over their cheap furniture…"

I pretended to laugh. "That actually sounds pretty good." Truth was: I was more than a little jealous at the thought of so many women getting to see him that evening, maybe even touch him, but I needed to get used to it since this was his job. And as long as I was the one heading backstage to help him work out his tensions after the fact…

"I'll book a car to come down and pick you up when it's time." He kissed me on the temple. "So you have a few hours to try out some of your new photography equipment, right?"

"Right." I nodded, looking over to the bags that had been

dumped against the bedroom door when we got back to his apartment. "Do you have to go now?"

"Yeah, pretty much. There's loads of set-up to do before the show kicks off. Since it's my first one back since the tour, they want to make it a big deal. A *huge* deal."

"I bet it's going to be amazing," I said, forcing a bright smile on my face. "You're a great dancer, Chad."

"Thank you." He planted a quick kiss on my lips, and flashed me a cocky smile. "But I'm a better lover."

I pretended to roll my eyes, and he sprang off the bed and headed to take a shower. As soon as I heard the shower running I chewed my lip uncertainly. Obviously, I'd known what he was when we met, so it wasn't like I could claim ignorance, or act like I hadn't known how he kept the cash rolling in, but I didn't expect him to go back to work this soon.

I guess, I had assumed that he would take some time off when the tour was over, that he would be able to dedicate a few more of his evenings to me, to the takeout and couch, and cuddling, and conversations. I guess I just wanted it to be like how it was last night.

I got to my feet, pulled on some clothes, and started unpacking everything that he'd bought for me. I wasn't in a place to be ungrateful given what he'd just done, and I was truly excited to get all this stuff out of the box and give it a go.

When he emerged from the shower, he stood there and watched me for I don't know how long – but when I turned, he had a smile on his face.

"You look so serious when you're reading," he remarked, touching my shoulder lightly as he brushed by me. I had my nose in the manual for one of the cameras he'd just bought me, trying to figure out how to get it to work.

"Yeah, well, if you were dealing with four thousand dollars' worth of equipment, you would too!" I called back as he went to put on his shoes and a coat.

"It's only money," he replied.

"It's not only money when you don't have it," I shot back.

He came back down and crouched on the floor with me, looking deep into my eyes. "Some things are far more important than money, Madison. I won't miss what I've spent this afternoon. I believe in you. So go take those photographs that you've always wanted to take."

I lost my voice then. I just nodded.

"I've called a car for you. They're going to send it around seven. And my housekeeper filled up the refrigerator while we were out today, so there's plenty of food. Help yourself, okay."

I wrinkled up my nose in disbelief. "Wait, you have a house-keeper too?"

He shrugged. "I'm lazy. I don't want to do my own cleaning."

"Holy hell," I shook my head. "Okay, I understand, I guess."

"So I'll see you at the show in a few hours?"

"Yep, you will," I promised. "Got to support my man when he takes his clothes of for a thousand other women, right?"

"Hey." He put his finger under my chin so I was forced to

look into his eyes. "I just want you to know that all those women might be there, but I'm only looking at you. All of it is just for you. Like it was the first time."

"And what about all the times before that?"

"Practice," he shot back, getting to his feet. "Okay, I have to go. I'll see you there soon."

"Good luck!" I called after him.

He smiled at me one last time before he headed out the door. Why should I feel down? Not only was going to get to go out tonight, I was going to sneak backstage for the first time in my life. So maybe this evening wasn't going to be a total write-off.

Then, before I could overthink my good fortune, I resolutely turned my attention back to my new camera equipment.

CHAPTER 23

MADISON

When the knock on the door came, I practically jumped out of my seat. The cab was here for me already. I had had all evening to get ready, but I wasn't sure I would ever feel totally prepared to lay eyes on Chad again.

I headed out to the cab with confident strides I did not feel. I slipped inside, and the driver took off at once. Closing my eyes, I leaned my head back against the leather seat. God, it felt good to have everything taken care of for me. I felt as though I could just disengage and relax for a change, not having to work myself into a lather about how I was going to get home at the end of the night and how much it was going to cost.

The car slowed in front of a huge theatre, lit up with giant posters of Chad and his team. I stared up at his shirtless image, and remembered the first night when I'd laid eyes on him for the very first time. The way my heart had drummed as though it already sensed: whatever was going to go down was big. Life-changing. The queue snaked out of the lobby and halfway down the street, and I frowned, wondering if I was going to have to wait in line with all the rest of the punters. But the driver continued down the street, turned into a side street, and pulled to a halt outside a nondescript back door.

He glanced at me in the rearview mirror. "This is where I was told to drop you off."

"Thanks," I called as I scrambled out of the car. Sure enough, moments later, the door opened and Chad stuck his head out. He glanced around to make sure no-one was on to us, before grabbing my hand and tugging me inside.

"Quickly," he murmured. "We don't have much time before I'm meant to go on."

"What in God's name are you doing?" I giggled, but he just pulled me down the corridor, his strides long and sure.

He bundled me inside his dressing room, closed the door shut behind me, and locked it quickly. Then he swung me up against the door, and kissed me hard. When he pulled back, my entire body felt as though it was on fire.

"Chad, what in God's name are you doing?" I demanded, struggling to catch my breath.

His hands moved over my waist and clamped around my hips. "I'm not waiting until after the show," he muttered.

"But your show starts in…" I trailed off. The way his hands were pulling at my dress was too much for me to keep thinking logically.

"In twenty minutes, yeah," he finished for me. "So I guess we better be fast, huh?"

"You're really serious?" I asked stunned. It was just the most unbelievable thing. No-one had ever been that overtaken with desire for me before, and it was almost impossible to get my head around the idea that someone like Chad would be that desperate for me.

"Deadly," he growled, as his mouth swooped down on mine. I wasn't about to resist. From the moment we met I was putty in his hands. Whatever he wanted to do to me, I was game. I wrapped my arms around him, our hands grabbing at each other's bodies, the time pressure burning in the back of my mind. Somehow the urgency made our coupling all the more hotter. I had never been fucked in such a hurry before and it felt amazing. His hand landed on the inside of my thigh. Rough, insistent, desperate

I was so lost in the moment a knock on the door, made me jump and try to pull away from him.

"Chad? Are you in there?" A voice called in. "We need you out now to start set-up."

"Maybe we should wait till after…" I whispered hoarse with fear and excitement, but Chad bent forward, caught my bottom lip between his teeth, and tugged on it.

"Or we just move this along a little faster," he muttered.

"Chad," the voice called.

Unable to move, my eyes widened. In one easy move, he turned me around so that I was facing the door. He picked up my hands and planted them both against the wood.

"Chad," the voice called again, this time sounding more uncertain.

Pushing my dress up, he pulled my panties down my legs.

I felt my knees start shaking. Was he really going to have sex with me while someone stood just outside the door. "Shouldn't you answer him first?"

"Why should I? He'll go away soon enough." I heard the zip of his jeans slide down, then the rip of the condom packet. I moaned when the tip of his cock pushed at the entrance of my pussy.

'You still want this right?" he growled close in my ear, as though there was any way in hell that I could have said no given the state he currently had me in.

"Yes," I panted, trying to keep my voice as quiet as I could. Hell, I couldn't believe I was doing this while there was someone right on the other side of that door, but it was so hot, knowing that he couldn't wait till after the show was done – that he had to have me right there, right then, no pauses, no breaks, no waiting. I pressed my hands against the wood, half so I could steady myself, and half so I could make sure that no-one burst in and caught us in the act. My pussy was already wet, my body reacting to the nervousness, the excitement, the arousal, and the desire for *him* all at once. I couldn't take this. I arched my back to push my pussy into the air towards him, begging him with every inch of my body to fuck me already.

"Chad, I can hear you in there," the voice said.

"God, you look beautiful like that," Cade said as he grabbed my ass and rammed into me in one, sharp motion.

"Oh, fuck," I gasped, louder than I intended.

The knock came from the other side of the door again.

"Chad, is that you? Are you in there? We need you out here right now!"

"Fuck off, Brian," Chad yelled back, and I could hear that ragged tension in his voice, as he tried to keep his irritation at Brian's insistence and deal with the fact that he was buried up to the hilt in my pussy. His cock felt so good at that angle, even bigger than it usually did, filling me up, my pussy spread wide trying to take all of him in.

"I'm not fucking leaving until you open this damn door," Brian said.

"You feel amazing inside me," I murmured.

"Fuck, you're so wet," he groaned, thrusting harder and deeper, reaching parts of me that I didn't even realize could be explored. He kept on fucking me with those deep, frantic strokes as though this was the only way he could release the tension in himself.

Someone was pounding on the door from the other side as I pushed back against him, teeth gritted. He moved his hand around me, found my clit instantly, and caressed it, his fingers slick from my wetness. He was about to go on stage, and his cock will still be wet from my pussy, and no-one would know a thing about it. The thought hit me like a ton of bricks, and I struggled to keep myself upright, legs trembling as pure lust overtook me. My brain dropped away and all that I could think about was how good he felt, how much I wanted him, how hard, how fast, how…

"Oh!" I gasped as the orgasm began to hit me, and he leaned forward to clap one hand over my mouth, the rest of the noises that I made were lost against his fingers. My pussy clenched around him, my clit pulsing beneath his fingers, as he thrust frantically into me a few more times as another knock came at the door.

"Chad, what the fuck is going on in there?" The voice sounded more agitated this time, but the pleasure had taken control of me. I could barely focus on it, my mind somewhere else entirely. "You need to come out, the show is about to start."

With a growl that seemed to come from somewhere deep inside of him, Chad exploded, hand still clamped over my mouth to keep me quiet – for some weird reason and I'm not in any way into bondage or BDSM, it was unbelievably sexy having him control me like that, even if it was more out of necessity than anything else. He held himself inside me as he finished, cock pushed so deep into me I wasn't sure the two of us would ever fully come apart again. But after a good long moment he pulled out of me, whipped the condom off, and did up his jeans.

"What do we do now?" I asked as I pulled up my underwear and dragged my dress down over it. My legs were trembling in the dangerously high heels I had picked out for the occasion. Chad wrapped an arm around my waist and kissed me deeply before I could tumble to the ground.

"I'm going to go out there and fucking stare them down and tell them never to bother me like that before a show again," he said. "And you're going to come out in five minutes and someone will be waiting outside to take you to your seat."

"But they'll all know what happened!" I gasped. Now that the lust had passed I couldn't imagine anything more mortifying, but he didn't seem bothered by it at all.

"I'm pretty sure they all already do," he pointed out. He held me close, as though letting me know that he wasn't going to let anyone near me or hurt me. "I have to go now, but I'll see you after the show, okay?"

I nodded.

Planting another quick kiss on my lips he opened for the door and stepped out. "What the fuck is wrong with you, banging on my door like that." I heard him say aggressively, before their footsteps and voices faded away.

Yeah, sure, this was a little embarrassing, but there was something kind of edgy about just walking out of here with my head held high as though none of this was a big deal, as though I hooked up with sexy male strippers in their dressing rooms all the time.

CHAPTER 24

MADISON

Chad did exactly as he had said he would. I opened the door five minutes later just as a slightly disgruntled-looking stagehand was coming up the corridor towards me.

"Miss Brooks?"

"That's me," I said, and to be honest, I didn't feel even a twinge of embarrassment as he took me on my walk of shame up to my seat. It was totally worth it. My seat was actually a whole box. So I got to look down on the stage in style. I wished I had a pair of those opera glasses, the kind that would let me peer down on him and see him in all his glory through a magnifying glass.

The audience was already in their seats, and I could feel the buzz of excitement radiating off them. I pressed my thighs together as a strange thrill ran through my body. Who would have ever imagined that someone like me would be the reason Subway Chad was late. I fantasized about getting to my feet and telling the audience that Chad had been too busy fucking me against a door to make it to the stage on time. If the show I attended in London was anything to go by, doing something like that would be tantamount to risking my life.

The stage was covered by a huge pair of red velvet curtains, but I could sense Chad down there. If I closed my eyes I could actually feel his energy, or maybe I was just being fanciful, and it was just his smell that had rubbed off on me that I was sensing in the air. Finally, the music changed, the announcer began to introduce the dancers and the curtains were pulled back. A deafening scream went up from the audience as a collection of dancers stepped out on to the stage, followed by Chad. He held his hand up as though acknowledging the attentions of all those women, and then he raised his gaze to meet mine. He flashed me a smile, one that I could tell was meant for me and me alone. My heart skipped a beat and I smiled back. His eyes lingered on me for another second, then he turned away, and they began their first dance routine.

It was easy to get caught up in the propulsive dance beat and pretend, for a little bit, that I wasn't a teenie-weenie bit jealous as I sat there and watched all those women below me openly lust after my man. Cat-calling, wolf-whistling, throwing their panties at the stage.

It was odd and a bit disconcerting.

I knew that he had sought out the best seat in the whole house for me, but I couldn't help feeling there a distance between us that wasn't there between him and the rest of the audience. I took my eyes off the stage and looked down at the women, reaching out for him desperately, and felt that attack of jealousy once more. I took a deep breath and exhaled slowly. Sure, I was going to have to get used to seeing this kind of thing if we were going to be together, but that didn't mean it had to be easy straight off the bat, did it?

I sat there and tried to appreciate the way that he danced. He was so good at it, he stood out even amongst the rest of the incredibly talented dancers. I should be happy I was with a guy who was such a success in his field. That was the way I had to look at this.

But it was hard, nearly impossible, given that I could feel the lusty thoughts these women had for him coming off them in waves. How could he go home with me when there were woman in that crowd who looked as though they had been plucked from the pages of a high fashion magazine? I knew the women in a sunshine city like Miami would be tanned and gorgeous, but this was ridiculous. Almost every one of those women would have turned heads back home. My insecurity nagged away at me, convincing me that Chad would prefer one of them more. I might have kicked Eleanor to the curb at last, but that didn't mean her unkind words and constant snipes hadn't left some kind of an impression on my psyche.

And then came the part of the show I'd been dreading.

The part where he pulled someone out of the crowd to dance up on. I held my breath as the announcement came. Of course, the crowd went wild and I watched with wide eyes, as he turned his gaze to the ladies in front of him. I knew it was selfish, but I wanted him to want me more than anyone else in the room. I wanted him to look up at me, to let me know with his eyes that he wished he could have had me down there instead, but my head knew it would have ruined the fantasy if he'd been so obviously into one of the women in the crowd.

He needed to make everyone feel as though they had a chance with him. That was the only way a show like this functioned as well as this one did.

Every woman in the audience tried to catch his attention with even more vigor than before. My hands clenched in my lap as I watched him move his finger across the audience. Who was he going to select? He went slow, taking his time, making the temperature in the room rocket, until finally he settled on a woman I couldn't quite see. I leaned forward to get a look at her, and my heart sank when I saw who he had selected.

He pulled her up on to the stage and started to dance against her. I did my best not to notice how much she looked like Eleanor. That had to be a coincidence. Surely? If he wanted Eleanor he would have picked her. How the hell did he manage to pick the only woman in this place with a passing resemblance to her. It was making my head pound.

I was relieved to note the way he danced against her wasn't quite as intense as the way he had moved against me, but still… The woman seemed to be loving it. She was touching him, touching his body, running her hands all over him like she owned him, and wanted the whole world to know. I knew I should have looked away, averted my gaze to keep from losing my mind, but I couldn't. I watched the two of them intently, every second of what they were doing to each other searing itself on to my memory, an ugly gash over the happy memories I had built with Chad so far.

The song came to a close, but the woman wasn't done with him yet.

She grabbed hold of his head, pulled herself towards him

and, to my horror, pressed her lips against him. The world seemed to slow down as the cheer of the crowd dulled in my ears. My fingernails dug into my palm as I tried to keep from screaming, *"Get your filthy hands off of my man."* It must have been two seconds before he pulled back, but it felt as though he had been making out with her for a lifetime.

He smiled gamely and waved her offstage, but that surge of jealousy that I had been keeping down overwhelmed me. I got to my feet and turned around blindly. I shouldn't have come here tonight. I didn't want to see other women rubbing up against him, kissing him, touching him, or even wanting him.

I couldn't handle it. I was not made for this kind of provocation. I just wanted to rush down there and punch that Eleanor lookalike's face in. I didn't want to be overdramatic, but I felt a sob rise up in my throat. What we had still seemed so delicate, so easily-broken, and I didn't like the way that it made me feel to have it ripped out from beneath me with just one woman's kiss.

I made my way backstage again, and slipped into his dressing room to wait for him. The staff waved me through without question. They must have noticed the look on my face and figured it was more trouble than it was worth to try and stop me. I sat at his dressing table, crossed my legs, and clasped my hands in my lap.

I could still hear the show go on outside, but all I could see in my head was that woman kissing Chad. The time sped by, as I replayed the image of that kiss again and again. I wanted, no, needed to stop myself, but I couldn't. Not until I had him in front of me again. Not until I could touch him and remind myself that he was mine.

Finally, the show came to an end, and I heard a bubble of voices heading down the corridor towards me as Chad easily chatted with his dancers.

"Good show," I heard them call out as he pushed the door open. He grinned widely when he saw me sitting at his dressing table. There was a sheen of sweat on his skin and he was breathing heavily.

"I'm so glad to see you," he said throatily, and pushing the door shut quickly, moved towards me. He kissed me, but I turned my head so that he hit my cheek instead of my lips. I could still see that woman kissing him, and I didn't even want to consider the fact that he was all hot and bothered because of her, or something else that had happened after I left. He pulled back, a furrow knitting his brow together.

"What's wrong?"

"I'm just tired," I replied. "The music was giving me a headache."

"You didn't enjoy the show?" His face dropped and he looked genuinely hurt. I knew he had no idea why I was acting like such a bitch, but I didn't particularly want to stop and explain myself. He was just doing his job and I was being unreasonable expecting him to understand why I was hurt, but I was too foggy with jealousy and rage to work out how to put that into words for him.

"I guess I'd just seen it all before," I replied.

He pressed his lips together, clearly keeping in a comment at my attitude. Then he exhaled and held his hand out to me. "Come on. Let's get home. I need to talk to you about something."

"Okay," I agreed, taking his hand. Despite it all, I did feel safe with his fingers locked with mine. There was something about his presence that made my body instinctively relax, even if I knew that the memory of what he had done with that woman was going to stay burned on my brain for a long time to come.

We caught a cab home, and he closed his eyes and leaned his head against the seat on the drive back. He was exhausted and confused by my mood. I felt even more like a bitch. I watched him surreptitiously, as though he might blink out of existence at any moment. None of this felt real. It was really hard for me to believe that someone like him, with the options that he had and the life that he led, would be even remotely interested in someone like me. But the fact was, my insecurity was starting to spill over and hurt the two of us as a couple, and I didn't like that one bit.

He opened his eyes, paid the driver, and gallantly helped me out of the car since it was clear that I was struggling to make a gracious exit in my killer heels. It was hard to remember that just a few hours earlier, the two of us had been having a frantic, hot-as-hell hook-up in his dressing room, unable to resist each other for a moment longer. That felt so far away now that I could hardly remember it.

"What was it you wanted to talk about?" I asked once he had collapsed on the couch. He ran a hand through his hair and yawned.

"My stage manager was talking to me during the intermission. He told me that there's a show across the state. They just had someone drop out, and they need someone else to step in for tomorrow night."

"And they want you guys?" I asked, resignedly.

He nodded.

I dropped my eyes. "And you said yes?"

"I haven't said yes yet, but it's a big gig for us all. Big stadium, new city, I'd be able to cancel my shows for the rest of the month cash-wise if I went…"

"You don't have to justify it to me," I shrugged. "It's your job. Go and do what you want."

He frowned. "Did I do something to piss you off?"

I looked up at him. What could I tell him? That the job he had chosen, the one that he was so clearly and obviously good at, the one that he had the day we met, was getting under my skin? No, that wasn't fair. He deserved to be able to do whatever he wanted, and not to have some woman he barely knew come swinging into his life and telling him to do things differently.

"No." I shook my head, and something cleared in his face.

"Do you want to come with me?" He asked, taking my hand. "It's just for a night, but it could be fun. We could—"

"No," I cut him out. I didn't want to see any more of his shows. It was bad for me, for us. I might have taken a step away from Eleanor and all her bad shit, but that didn't mean that the impression she'd left had faded yet. I was still too insecure to handle seeing gorgeous women grinding up on him on a nightly basis. Maybe I would even get the nerve to tell him one day, but for now, I just wanted him to see me as the carefree, fun girl who could drop everything and move across the world with him at a moment's notice. Who wouldn't want to be that woman, after all?

He stared at me with surprise.

I forced a smile. "I'm going to stay back here and get started on my photography.

"Oh, okay." He licked his lip. "Are you sure?"

"Certain," I confirmed, and got to my feet. "Here, let's go to bed. I'm tired and I'm guessing the jetlag is catching up on you."

"Sure," he agreed, and followed me into the bedroom. I headed to the bathroom as he got undressed, and looked at myself in the mirror. I needed to get my shit together, because the way I was acting now just wasn't going to cut it. I had a gorgeous guy, who had made it clear every chance he got that he was crazy into me, and I needed to start believing it.

CHAPTER 25

CHAD

The show was in a couple of hours, but I wanted to talk to Madison first. Ever since I kissed her goodbye while she was still sleepy and warm in bed, I felt as though there was some part of me missing, some part of me I left behind in Miami.

I drummed my fingers on the table in front of me and waited for my laptop to boot up. It was already getting to my nerves, this long-distance thing. Maybe if she hadn't been so off with me last night, I wouldn't feel like smashing something. I made the wrong decision to come here. As if I needed the money. It was just hurt pride. We were getting on so well until…for no reason at all, she became cold and distant.

When chicks have played that game with me in the past they were out of my life so fast they left a cloud of dust. But with Madison, I can't even imagine asking her to walk. I realized now that I should have stayed and worked out whatever it was that was bothering Madison. I was new at this relation-ship thing, but I learned fast. I would never make that mistake again.

When my laptop sprang to life I pulled up the video calling app I downloaded at the airport and called her. She was kind of brisk in her text messages. I didn't know her well enough to tell if that was just how she was in texts, or if she was still pissed at me. I couldn't figure why she would have been though. Nothing happened. She came to the show last night, and everything had seemed fine, actually more than fine, to me until after the show. Maybe she was embarrassed about me dancing, the same way my parents were.

Fortunately, before I could short-circuit my brain by over-thinking the issue, she answered my call and sprang up on the screen in front of me. As soon I clapped eyes on her my chest swelled with happiness. She wearing one of my old T-shirts and I got a glimpse of her bare thigh. She looked homey and comfortable and also really, really fuckable.

"Hey," she greeted me, a little shyly.

"Hey," I replied. "You look super sexy."

"Oh, come on." She looked down at her clothes. "I just stole this because it smells of you."

This was more like the Madison I knew. I grinned. "It suits you, you should keep it." I changed my voice to one of mock severity. "Though you're not allowed to wear pants with it, understand?" I said with mock severity.

"Yes, sir." She saluted me and giggled. "Hang on let me get comfortable." I watched her cross her fantastic legs, and arrange her phone so that she could sit comfortably and talk to me.

"So what have you been up to today?" I asked, leaning back on the bed and pulling the laptop up onto my stomach.

"I've just been tinkering around with the photography stuff you got me." She smiled. "It's been really fun."

"You know, I never asked you what kind of stuff you want to take pictures of," I said. "What have you been shooting?"

"Uh, well, I thought I would start with fruit and vegetables. That way I can play with lighting and practice filters."

"Did you take some photos?"

"Mmm."

"Want to show me?"

She reached for something off-camera, and came back into the camera's view holding a stack of prints. "I took these…"

She held them up to the camera one-by-one. I looked at them all carefully, giving them my full attention. I wanted her to know that whatever was important to her was important to me, too. I was surprised by how good they were. Not that I thought they would be bad, but if she was just starting out, I didn't expect this amount of deftness and skill. I had worked with a few photographers in my day, taking promo shots and the like, and the way that she had used the light to bring out the details on the various pieces of fruit and vegetables was actually very artistic and delicate.

"They're really good," I said enthusiastically when she put the pictures away. And they were – but now that I had seen them, I had something in my head, something else entirely. She must have seen the glint in my eye, because she raised her eyebrows expectantly.

"What is it?" she asked, a little breathless already. Being apart from her was hard, physically, because all I wanted to do was walk through the screen, scoop her up, toss her down on to the bed and fuck her right then and there.

"There was a cucumber in one of those pictures, right?" I asked.

She nodded slowly, her tongue flicking out over her bottom lip.

Damn, I practically groaned at the frustration of not having her right there in front of me to do what I wanted with. "You still got it?"

"Yeah," she said slowly, glancing off-camera. "Why?"

"Did you wash it?"

"Yeah."

"Good. Go get it," I ordered.

She shot me a funny look before getting to her feet and doing as she was told. She returned with the cucumber, a good seven inches long and thick, and sat back down in front of the camera again. I could see in her face that she had already figuring out where I was going with this.

"So," she raised her eyebrows expectantly, a flicker of a wicked smile passing over her face. "What do you want me to do with ... this?"

"Lie back and position the camera so I can see all of you," I demanded.

She did as she was told, shifting the camera so I could see her from her toes to half-way up her neck. I could have asked her to adjust the camera and get her face into focus too, but somehow the pretense of anonymity made it even more delicious.

My mouth began to water as my gaze ran down her curves. I was desperate to run my hands over the thickness of her thighs, her ass, but I would have to make do with memory for now. I reached down to massage my erection through my pants. I need to find a little relief after all this time.

"And?" she prompted innocently, still holding the cucumber. I knew that she knew what I wanted, but she was making me say it, and that was somehow the hottest thing in the world.

"Take off your panties and spread your legs."

She obeyed at once, sliding her thumbs beneath the silk of her underwear and slipping them off her legs. Even the shape of her pussy, it was almost too much to handle. I slipped my hand inside my pants and began to stroke myself.

"Spread open," I ordered.

She bent her knees and let them fall sideways to the floor. I could see her bush, that fluff of hair that led down to her pussy, and the glistening pink flesh between. It looked so sweet, it was all I could do not to reach out and touch the screen, as if I could feel her through it. I was overtaken by the desire to see what happened next.

"Like this?" she asked, and I could hear the tremble of insecurity in her voice even though I couldn't see it in her eyes. There was something between us I had never felt before, that I had never felt with anyone, definitely not with any of those girls I got up on stage with.

"Use the cucumber on yourself," I ordered, and I could see her stiffen with nerves when the words actually came out of my mouth. She had obviously never done anything like this before. Slowly, she lifted it and guided it towards her slit. My breath was coming harder as I stroked my cock with more purpose. I could almost feel her pussy around my cock as she pressed the tip of the cucumber against her pussy. I watched it slip inch by inch inside of her with almost painful slowness. Her body tensed up as she pushed it into herself, as if she was not yet used to the feel of it inside her, but soon she began to relax, and I heard the softest little moan. I imagined her mouth parting, her lips pushing forward almost in a pout, and another strong surge of desire rushed through me and I had to grit my teeth to stop myself from coming.

I never took my eyes off her once as she pushed the dark green vegetable inside her, grinding back against it, lifting and writhing her hips. When her other hand reached over to adjust the camera, my mouth fell open. My whole screen was just her pussy stretched with a cucumber.

She must have been watching to see my reactions, as it seemed to embolden her. Her hand appeared and started to stroking and playing with her clit in time with her thrusts. And after that she matched my reaction with one of her own. Every time I let out a little growl of pleasure at the show she was putting on, she would double down, thrusting deeper, harder, or faster.

She made a little sound like a meow, and I knew she was close to coming. Even though we only just hooked up, I knew from the way her body tensed, or the noises she made when she was getting ready to climax. I could even have described the exact look in her eyes at that moment.

"Ah!" she cried as she found her release.

I could imagine her head tilting back as she came suddenly, her legs twitching and trembling. The cucumber was still thrust halfway inside of her, and her pretty little cunt was gushing. The sight of it was enough to get me off. I came on the expensive hotel sheets.

We both stayed still for a moment or two, coming back down to earth, catching our respective breath. She slid the cucumber out of her, ducked her head back into frame, and slumped back against the sofa behind her.

"I've never done anything like that before," she confessed, her eyes still dark and heavy-lidded, but kind of awed, as if she couldn't believe she'd just done something that filthy.

"Me neither," I replied. "I guess you just bring it out in me."

"I should get rid of this, I suppose," she laughed, pointing off-camera to what I assumed was the cucumber.

"Absolutely. The next thing going into your pussy is my cock."

She blushed.

"Madison?"

"What?"

"I want you to know you looked amazing. I won't be able to sleep tonight thinking of you with your cucumber."

"Thanks, I think," she murmured, her eyes shining. She checked the time and frowned. "Uh, so, what time is it there? Have you performed yet?"

I shook my head and looked at the clock above the television. "No, but it's probably time for me to go and get ready," I admitted reluctantly. "I'll see you tomorrow though, right? I'll be back as early as I can. I'll text you when I'm nearly there."

"Good luck with the show tonight," she replied, and I could see her jaw had clenched slightly, her lips pressed together when she finished speaking, as though there was something she was trying to hide.

"Are you sure everything's—"

"Everything's fine," she cut me off. "I'll see you tomorrow. Good luck with the show tonight."

"Alright, goodnight. I—"

Before I could exchange some of those sweet nothings that girls normally crave to hear, she had clicked off the call. I stared at the screen for a moment. Maybe she had hung up by accident. She was never normally that abrupt in person. I waited for her to reconnect, but nothing came through. It was clear that was her goodbye. It was also clear something was wrong.

I lay there for a good ten minutes thinking about our situation before I reluctantly climbed out of bed and started getting ready for the show. I had to put on a good performance, and I sure as hell wasn't going to let down the crowd out there tonight, but tomorrow I was getting to the bottom of Madison's problem.

CHAPTER 26

MADISON

My hands were shaking as I hung up. I felt like a complete and utter bitch. I felt as if I was ruining everything and I hated myself for doing it, but I couldn't control my emotions.

I had never been so sharp with anyone in my life, not even Eleanor who had dropped me in the shit from a very high place. I pressed my palms on my heated face. To think he had reached out and called me and let me know that he was thinking of me. Why? Why was I reacting in this completely irrational way? Why couldn't I be more cool about it all? It was just his job. What did I expect? Him to leave his work for me when we just met a few days ago?

Then I thought of him going to his show and an image of Eleanor's lookalike rubbing herself against him last night popped into my mind. She had kissed him, for goodness sake, and he had taken more than a split-second to push her off.

I remembered how I had felt when he picked me out from

the crowd. As if it was the confirmation that he too had felt the buzzing electricity between us. Maybe all the women he pulled up on stage felt that way too. My stomach twisted into a knot.

Maybe he always zeroed in on women like me, a little down on her luck and romantically insecure. He pulled us from the crowd, danced on us, and made us feel like princesses for the first time in our lives.

And if the woman responded in a way that was encouraging like I had, would he go find her at the bar afterwards? Would he take her back to his hotel room like he did with me? Jesus, he could be doing God knows what with God knows who right now.

I jumped to my feet. I was going to be stuck here all evening by myself driving myself crazy. I had to stop torturing myself like this and get a hold of my thought pattern, or I was going to find myself on a plane back to my little apartment in London. What a laugh Eleanor would have then.

I poured myself a drink from the cabinet in the kitchen, a vodka-soda. Something light. If I was going to keep his attention with all those girls throwing themselves at him, then I was going to need to lose weight, and that meant less wine and beer and more in the way of these boring, low-calorie drinks.

No.

I slammed the drink on the bar counter so hard, liquid slopped out and flowed onto the shiny granite. I took a few deep breaths. I couldn't think like that. He was with me because he wanted to be, not because I had forced him, or because he was being charitable. He could have had any woman that night, including Eleanor, but he chose me.

Me.

With all my faults.

Convinced by Eleanor and reiterated by myself, I had allowed myself to get stuck in a feedback loop that I was nothing more than a fatty destined for a life alone. According to Eleanor no good-looking man could possibly be interested in me. The best I could ever hope for was a man with little prospects who would be willing to settle on me because I was a good and understanding person.

I had believed it all. Even after I had seen what she had done that one time at the bar we had gone to. When I overheard her telling a guy that I was actually married with two kids so he shouldn't waste his time with me. I had liked him too, but when I had cornered her she said she had done it for my own good. She knew his kind. He was no good.

In fact, for as far back as I could remember she had played this long game of convincing me that she was the hot one and I was the ugly best friend. Chad had upended that, and I guess, it was taking a while for it to sink in. So I repeated the fact.

Chad chose me.

I poured the vodka-soda down the sink, cleaned the mess I had made, then made myself a real drink. I took a sip and rationally went through what happened last night. Yes, the woman had rubbed herself against him, and yes, he had not pushed her away as quickly as I would have wanted, but if I was reasonable then it was obvious it was because he couldn't. If he had pushed her off

149

immediately or as if he found her unattractive, the premise of the whole show would have been ruined. The fantasy that he was available to all those women would have been shattered.

I finished my drink and poured myself another. I let my gaze fall on the photography equipment I had been messing about with all day. I remembered how excited he'd been to buy it for me. How thrilled he had seemed to be setting me up with the kind of life here that I had always dreamed about. Even my deep insecurity couldn't pretend that he did that with every woman he danced with.

I felt this swell in my chest. I didn't recognize the emotion at once, but it was strong and solid. Stronger than anything I'd ever felt for any man. In my heart, I knew it was love. Of course, I wouldn't say it to him yet, but I was glad it was him.

Chad treated me as if he couldn't believe his eyes, as if he had found the most beautiful woman in the world. He was funny, charming, talented, ambitious, tinges of his old bad-boy past clinging to him. He was the man I would have written out for myself if I could, filling in each detail carefully, one at a time. And now that I was with such a man, was it so unusual that I would question my unbelievable luck? A man so perfect, so desirable, wanting me?

I spent the rest of the night learning how to Photoshop. Every time I started thinking of him I'd shake the thoughts from my mind. Of a woman climbing all over him, touching his chest, his stomach, his legs, his ass? Was there so much raw sexual passion in the air that he would need to work it off with her afterwards? Would he bring someone else back to his dressing room, work out his tension on her? I simply pushed it back and turned my mind back to my work.

But after a while I became mentally exhausted with the effort. I got out of the apartment and walked along the beach. The sound of the waves soothed me and I took off my sandals and stood in the cool water. It was so beautiful and peaceful, but I didn't feel happy.

I knew a difficult time lay in front of me. I loved Chad, but I hated having to share him. And I knew I wasn't a good enough actress to pull of pretending his job didn't matter to me. When I got in I lay in bed and stared at the ceiling, the smell of him was still fresh on the sheets. I hoped he would call again, but he didn't. I got out of bed and poured myself a generous measure of Vodka. I stared out of the window at the restless waves and waited for him to call me. I waited until nearly two in the morning.

Tears stung my eyes. I really thought he would call.

Being here while he was away performing was worse than being at the performance and watching him with a woman. I missed him so much I cried myself to sleep. The last thought I had, before my mind drifted into merciful sleep, was you're going to get hurt, you know.

The first thing I did when I woke up the next day was turn my head and look at the empty pillow next to me. God, how I missed him. I checked my phone and there was no message. It actually made me feel sick to see he had not called or even left a text.

I pulled myself out of bed and ate some toast for breakfast. My stomach was a little swirly from the booze so I took my time, chewing slowly as I cast my eye around the apartment. I wondered how long it had taken him to save for a place like this. It was so masculine and immaculate it felt as though there wasn't room for me in it.

I wondered where he was and why he did not call. I stared out of the window at the ocean. A dog ran past. Its fur was flying and it looked so happy. This should have been the most incredible week of my life, and yet I was letting those insecure voices whisper into my ear and ruin everything. There could have been any number of reasons why he did not call. I wasn't going to let myself jump to any conclusions. I did enough of that last night.

I decided on a shower, hoping the hot water would be enough to wash away my hangover. It did kind of help. I sat on the edge of the bed, my hair pulled up into a towel and wearing an old shirt of his, and thought about what I wanted to do for the day. The photography equipment stood in the living room, but until I knew where he was it didn't have any pull at all for me. Maybe I should get out of the house. Get a coffee or something. It would help take my mind away from brooding about him.

I was about to get up and put on some clothes to go out when the door opened. My heart leapt, and then twisted up in my chest; it was him, no doubt about that, but I wasn't sure what I was going to see in his eyes.

"Hey," he called into the house.

"I'm in here," I croaked.

"Sorry I didn't message you, my phone ran out of battery and I left my charger at the hotel," he said as he entered the bedroom, but as soon as he saw me, his face dropped. Was I that obvious? He stood for a moment looking at me. Neither of us said anything, then he came and sat next to me, and wound his arms around me. God, help me, but I noticed that he smelled different than normal. I tried to tell myself it was just the hotel soap and shampoo, but my rattled brain wouldn't take another woman off the list of possibilities. Instinctively, I drew away from him.

"Hey, what's going on?" he asked gently.

I jumped to my feet and began to pace. "I'm so sorry," I blurted out, shaking my head. "I know I've been off the last couple of days, I just feel…" I trailed off. He deserved an explanation, but I felt such a fool. Unable to meet his gaze, I turned and looked to the ocean. He said nothing while I took control of my thoughts once more. Chad sat in silence, waiting for me to explain myself.

"I'm really glad you're back," I confessed, sitting down next to him on the bed and leaning against him.

"But…" He wrapped his arms around me once more, pulling me close, and he pushed his face into my hair, inhaling deeply.

"No, buts. I'm really glad you're back."

"Well, I'm really glad to be back too," he murmured, and the vibration of his voice ran through my entire body.

"You want to tell me what's up?" he prompted softly.

I swallowed hard. He had been good to me and I owed him this. I lifted my head from his chest, looked him in the eye, and just came out with the truth. "I'm just scared," I confessed.

"Of what?"

"Your job."

He frowned.

"When you picked me out of the crowd and pulled me up on stage, I'd never felt anything like it before in my life. And I thought it was special. Nothing like that had ever happened to me, but then last night, I saw the way you were with those women at the show." I bit my lip. "And I realized it wasn't special, after all."

He shook his head. "What are you talking about?"

"I mean. This is what you do for living. Pick women out of crowds, dance with them and fulfill their fantasies. So I don't know if you're...if it's just me or if you felt a real connection with me," I admitted at last.

He sat there in stunned silence, and I knew that he was hurt by what I was saying. "Madison," he finally explained, "I've never felt the connection I have with you for anyone. And I've danced so many shows, so many women, I can't even begin—"

"Yeah, I don't need reminding," I interrupted quickly. I couldn't to go there. One issue at a time was enough. I was not ready to show him what a green-eyed monster I had become.

He closed his eyes for a moment. "I'm sorry. I just want you to know, this isn't normal for me. I've never done this before. I've never met anyone like you before."

"I'm sorry too," I apologized. "I know that it's not fair for me to be upset about your job. You were doing it when I met you, I can't get...I can't be mad about this."

"You can't help the way that you feel." He pulled me tighter against his body, as though he didn't want me to get away. "I know it's hard to handle. You should have seen my dad's face when I told him."

"You said you got into it to piss off your dad. You think he's pissed off enough now?" I was smiling wryly when I said it, to let him know that I was only kidding. I didn't actually expect him to give it up, but he knitted his brows together and sighed.

"You know, I've been doing this for so long that I don't even…I couldn't even imagine my life without it, you know?"

"I know. I'm not asking you to give up your job or anything, obviously. It's just something I have to work out in my head. Just be a little patient with me, okay."

"It's just a job, Madison."

"I know." I nodded. "It's just a job to you, I get that, but seeing you kiss those women—"

"Like an actor kissing someone for a part," he cut me off. "It doesn't mean anything. In fact, sometimes, I can't wait for the show to be over. I only care when I kiss you."

I swallowed. "I couldn't help but think, you know, when I saw that girl kiss you on stage that, it was just the same as it was when you were kissing me," I admitted quietly, completely embarrassed that I was being so honest about my insecurity, but he was being honest with me and he deserved my sincerity to.

"It's not like that," he said urgently. "You have to understand that."

"What if one day, a woman makes you feel the way I did?" I asked. "Will you go with her?"

He closed his eyes. "It's never going to be like that again," he promised.

"What if the shoe was on the other foot, and I was pulling a man up from the audience and grinding myself against him."

His is jaw clenched so tight the muscles at the side of his face jumped violently. "I'd fucking kill that bastard."

"See what I mean now."

"Okay, okay. You made your point," he conceded. "But I want you to understand something. People like you…"

"People like me are scared that they've just given up everything in their lives to follow someone they don't know across the world," I finished for him. I needed him to convince me that I'd made the right choice once and for all.

He touched his finger to my chin and drew my face round to his and looked deep into my eyes. "People like you come once in a lifetime. Some men are stupid, they need time to convince themselves and 'give up' their freedom, not me. I've had more than my share of women. And I can tell you, meaningless sex, no matter how exciting, just leaves you feeling empty."

"You're not just saying this to make me feel better."

"How about this?" he suggested, running his hands through his hair, and suddenly I saw how tired he was. To arrive this early he must have caught a flight in the early morning hours. I was so grateful that he was willing to sit up with me and make sure that I was feeling okay above anything else.

"I only started doing this because I wanted to piss off my family and make some quick money." He gestured around at the apartment. "Well, mission accomplished. I only have a couple of months on my contract left, and after that... honestly, I'm ready to give it up. It's been fun, don't get me wrong, but it's not worth hurting you over."

My eyes nearly popped out of my head. "What?"

He shrugged. "I don't want to hurt you. The last thing in the world I want to do is that."

"You're serious?" I gaped at him. I could hardly believe what I was hearing, feeling.

"Yeah, I'm serious," he replied.

"But I'd hate you to give up something you love because of me."

"I've been thinking. Its crossed my mind the last year that I should move into something else. I mean, I'm not getting any younger. I can't be doing this for the rest of my life, can I?"

"Are you sure?" I asked quietly.

"I'm not a kid anymore. I'm ready to start something new," he replied firmly. "You're just the spur I need to make it happen."

"What, dancing into your sixties?" I teased. "I don't know, I'm sure there's a market for that."

"I'm not sure I want to find out." He pulled a face, and I realized that my hands were trembling with happiness. In the past, when I'd been vulnerable like this, I had been so used to being shot down, or told that I was acting crazy, and for him to listen to me and hear what I was saying and go out of his way to fix things...it made me feel so valued. So loved.

There was that word again. I pushed it to the back of my mind. We both needed some time yet. I managed a smile. "So, a couple more months and you'll be done with it?" I confirmed.

He nodded. "I promise. I want to start my own business. Do something that I can pass on to my kids, you know?"

"Kids?" I raised my eyebrows, and he grinned.

"Maybe," he replied, and bounced to his feet. "Come on, let's go out for a while. I want to celebrate."

"Celebrate what?" I grinned, taking his hand and letting him pull me to my feet. "We haven't done anything yet."

"Celebrate the fact that we're together," he replied simply.

"Aren't you tired? Don't you want to sleep?"

"I'll sleep when I'm a grandpa."

And I couldn't keep the smile from my face as I thought about what was to come. A couple more months, and I would have him all to myself. Only a couple more months. The world felt a hell of a lot brighter than it had done before he walked through the door like a ray of sunshine.

Now I knew, without doubt, that Chad was as serious about this as I was.

CHAPTER 27

MADISON

A Month Later

"Sasha?" I said, as soon as my sister answered the phone.

"Maddy, what's wrong?" my sister asked worriedly, and I wondered if I was that transparent. I felt as though I needed two weeks of sleep, ten drinks, and at least a full session of a total-body massage to even begin to feel better again.

I took a deep breath and exhaled it slowly. I still hadn't figured out how I was going to tell my sister that I was pregnant. It was the most reckless thing I had ever done in my life and she would be shocked. As far as she was concerned, I was just having a good time, and one day I would pack my bags and go back to England. This was going to come as a shocker.

I only found out yesterday. Something felt off, but I had

convinced myself I was just paranoid. It was all down to moving to a new country and getting used to the weather, and the food, and the different time zone.

Chad was still dancing, but I had convinced Chad going to his shows would only make my jealousy worse and render the next couple of months harder. He had accepted that, even though I was pretty sure he was a little pissed we didn't get to repeat that hot hook-up in his dressing room again. When he went to work I spent those evenings hiding out in the apartment and pretending like none of it was happening.

I worked on my photography, slowly getting a grasp on how to use all the equipment and software he had purchased for me. To take my mind off what he was getting up to I'd even set up an Instagram account so I could start sharing some of my photographs and then when he came home I tried to be sexy and remind him that I was his woman, but something had changed between us.

Chad was being a little off with me these last few days. I knew it was not my imagination. Something was definitely up. The other day I walked into the room and he was talking to someone on the phone, but when he saw me he ended the call and pretended it was one of the guys from the show.

I knew it was not.

It hurt me that he lied to me, but I couldn't confront him about it. Of course, then I didn't know I was already pregnant, but I guess, having my hormones screwed up made me a coward. I played along and didn't push him to tell me who he was really talking to. I told myself I would start to withdraw my feelings from him. Slowly, I would make myself fall out of love with him, and prepare to return home. Back to where I belonged. Sasha was right. It was just a fling and the sooner I saw it as that, the faster I could get on with my life.

Now I wish I could go back to a time when the only thing I had to worry about was leaving Chad. When I realized that my period was late it hit me with a gut-wrenching pain that there was something else going on too. Something scary. Something bigger than I'd ever imagined.

I snuck out to the drugstore and grabbed a pregnancy test, and came home and sat on the bathroom floor in horror for a whole hour. Then I went out and bought another. I stared at those two blue lines in disbelief for ages.

We had been so careful. The only thing I could think of was the condom must have split during one of our marathon sessions.

By the time that I accepted that I was, in fact, pregnant, I was three tests deep and so lost in panic I could hardly see straight. But Chad was coming home in an couple of hours and I had to accept it and deal with it.

I was pregnant, Chad was the father, and I was convinced he had already moved on, found someone else. I had never felt smaller or more insignificant in my entire life. My heart ached with pain for me and my unborn child. I wanted with all my heart to keep my baby. I was so far from home. So far from my support system. I didn't want to be a single mother on my own with no way to support myself. I threw away the tests and fortified myself.

I had my pride.

To my surprise Chad noticed something was wrong right off the bat. He practically followed me around the house, trying to get me to tell him what was going on in my head, but I pretended everything was fine and I was just a little home-sick. He backed off then, as if I had burnt him, or maybe it was relief. If I was homesick, maybe I would decide to go home. I was in the shower getting ready for bed, when I real-ized that it was the most attention he'd paid to me in days.

My heart sank as the reality of my situation began to sink in. My man, who was so totally into me and could not get enough, for one reason or another, seemed to have gone off of me, and I was pregnant with his baby. I had to face up to my shit, but that didn't mean I had to do it alone. I had Sasha. And I was not giving her up.

"Sasha, I'm pregnant," I blurted out.

The only indication she was still at the other end of the line was the sound of her sharp gasp after the words came out of my mouth.

"What?" She sounded as shocked as I had felt when I had found out.

The words were like a jolt of electricity through my nervous system, pain and panic shivering across my skin. I felt myself begin to choke up all over again. I had been so emotional, and finally telling someone the truth was bringing all my pain to the fore. I forced myself to breathe deeply; in and out, in and out. It helped, and I went on. "I just found out last night," I admitted. "I've been feeling kind of weird, and I just…I knew something was up, so I took a test."

"Just one?" Her voice was full of hope.

"Nope. Three," I admitted. "I wanted to be sure, and I am."

"And it's Chad's?" She prompted me.

"Of course," I shot back, irritated that she would even think otherwise. "I haven't been with anyone else since I got here."

"Oh God. Are you going to keep it?"

"Pretty much, yeah," I replied.

"Does he know yet?"

"No. I'm not even sure how I'm meant to tell him, Sasha. I… things have been a bit weird between us the last couple of weeks…"

I traced my mind back, to the first time that I had noticed there was something off about Chad. It had been when he came back from one of his shows. I had tried to tell him about a famous photographer who had started following me on Instagram, but he just listened quietly, showing no enthusiasm at all. When I was finished he yawned, made some placating noises and went off to have a shower.

"Weird like how?" Sasha prompted, clearly worried. "Madison, tell me what's going on. He not…"

"No, no, it's not like he's doing anything terrible," I assured her quickly. "It's just … when I first came over, he was all over me. He took me out places, he couldn't do enough for me. He was always asking my opinion, how I was doing…"

"And not so much anymore?" she finished bluntly. She had never been one to hold back, and I figured that right now that was what I needed. Someone to come straight out and tell me the truth, even if it felt like a kick in the teeth to hear it.

"Yeah," I admitted. "Not so much anymore. He's been colder. He comes home and goes straight to bed. I walked in on him making a call the other day and he hung up right away, like he didn't want me to hear what it was about, and then he was all cuddly with me right after like he was trying to make up for something."

"Mads, is it possible you're reading too much into this?" she asked. "That kind of clawing passion doesn't last and maybe this is just you guys settling in to the relationship or something."

"Maybe," I sighed. "But … but it's too different."

"You think he's gone off you?" she pressed, and there was a hint of anger in her voice, like she had every intention of marching all the way across the ocean, and giving him a piece of her mind unless he got his act together.

My mouth turned down at the corners. "You know, I really think he has. He's been staying out late after the shows are over. I check on social media and I can see that people are coming out, and yet it's always a good couple of hours before he actually turns up back at the apartment."

"Hmm…" She sounded wary.

"I mean, I don't know anyone else in this whole damn country, Sasha. Maybe he's just getting bored of carrying me. I should have tried to get a job or something."

"Hey, it was him who dragged you over there, remember?"

"I know, but maybe he's just changed his mind or found someone else."

"And now you're pregnant,"

"Now I'm pregnant," I repeated miserably.

"Are you sure you want to keep it?"

"Yes," I breathed. "Yes, I'm going to keep it."

"Holy shit, Madison!"

She almost sounded so shocked that I couldn't help but splutter with laughter.

"What the hell are you laughing at?" she demanded. "You know this is serious, right?"

"Oh, I know," I finally caught my breath, the smile fading from my face. "It's just that…I don't think I can handle all of this without laughing a little at how crazy it is, you know?"

"I know," she replied gently.

I felt the laughter bubble over into something else inside of me. I wanted to be near her so badly. I needed my sister to help guide me through this, but she felt as though she was on the other side of the universe to me. Tears began to roll down my cheeks and I dashed them away quickly with the back of my hand. Crying wasn't going to get me anywhere; I had to come up with something practical to do and quick, before my brain became too addled by hormones to do anything else.

"I think I need to come back to London," I said quietly. I couldn't believe I was saying those words out loud. Only a few weeks ago, I had been so cocksure I was going to make a new life for myself in Miami. I had even gone online to research what it would take to get my citizenship and everything. But now, Chad felt a million miles away. I had this baby to think of and all I wanted was some space to breath and think again.

"Don't cry, Maddy. We'll work it out," she choked.

"I'm not," I said, the tears falling without restraint now. She couldn't see me, but even if she could I didn't much care to hide the way I was feeling anymore. It felt as though there was a void deep inside of me, one that only Chad could fill. But he had left me alone to lose myself in it while he went out and danced up on God knows who.

"You're going to tell him about the baby, aren't you?" she pressed. "I know it's going to be tough, but he has a right to know."

"Yeah, I'm going to tell him eventually," I assured her. "I just don't want to be in Miami when I do it. I don't want him to think that I'm trying to trap him with this thing, you know?"

"But you're not," she reminded.

I closed my eyes. "I know that, but I don't know what he'll believe. If he doesn't want me then I don't want him to stay with me just because of the baby." It felt crazy to say that, when a mere month before I'd been sure I understood Chad inside and out. But I had to admit that things were different now. The man I'd been so sure I had an unbreakable connection with was gone. And a stranger stood in his place.

"So you're going to come back here, then tell him?" she asked incredulously.

"Yeah, that's the plan." I sighed deeply, my voice wavering. "That's what I want."

"Oh, Mads," Sasha replied. "I'm so sorry. I wish I could be there with you now."

"Meet me at the airport?"

"Anything you want," she promised.

"I'll let you know when I'm getting in, okay?"

"Okay." She was so sure I was making a crazy decision when I left, but she was still my sister and that meant standing by me even when the choices I had made had revealed themselves to be dumb as all hell.

"I'll talk to you soon," I finished up quickly, as I felt another bubble of emotion threaten to overwhelm me.

"Okay, bye. I'm here. Call me anytime."

"Okay."

"Love you, Mads."

"Love you too," I replied. I hung up and sank into the couch behind me. That was when the grief really hit me. Oh, sweet Jesus, I would be leaving all of this behind. Leaving it all behind to walk into a life I had never imagined for myself.

A life without Chad.

A life alone.

CHAPTER 28

MADISON

"Why are we going out to dinner tonight?" I asked, shifting uncomfortably back and forth in the seat of the cab. I wasn't sure whether it was the pregnancy, or just nerves, but I didn't want to be in a public place with him.

"I have a surprise for you."

I felt my heart sink. Surprise? What kind of surprise? I really hoped that he wasn't going to try and pull anything big, because I needed to tell him that I planned to fly back to London next week. And as a matter of fact, I had picked tonight as the do-or-die night.

It was just my luck that he had come back from rehearsals with a big-ass grin on his face and a desire to hit the town. I did try to talk him out of it, but he had insisted and of course, I had talked myself into believing that perhaps this was for the best. If the two of us were out and about when I broke the news to him, neither of us were likely to make a scene. Or rather, an audience would mean I was less likely to end up in floods of tears.

I sat in the taxi across from him, one hand on my stomach and the other clenched into a fist at my side. I couldn't believe that this was really happening. I wanted nothing more than to back out, than to find some way to rewind to the place that we had been at just a few weeks before, when I had felt myself toppling over in love with him and had been sure that he felt the same way too.

That said, as I sat slightly apart from him and surreptitiously watched him out of the corner of my eye. I was sure I saw a flicker of the old Chad. There was a small smile playing at the corner of his lips, as though he was sitting on a secret, and I couldn't help wondering what it could be. Whatever it might be, I could almost guarantee that it wouldn't come anywhere close to what I was going to drop on him.

"Where are we headed?" I asked.

He reached over and squeezed my hand, and despite myself, I felt a tingle of excitement at his touch.

"You'll see," he grinned mysteriously, as he leaned over and planted a quick kiss on my temple. I looked away in confusion. Why did he have to be like this now, when I was so close to leaving? Of course, it was possible that I was imagining everything and searching for any excuse to stay, but I was sure that he was acting differently than he had been the past couple weeks.

He had spent so much extra time out rehearsing and performing I was sure he was either deliberately staying away from me, or pursuing some extracurricular that he didn't want me to know about. True, I didn't have much experience with men, but when someone goes from smoking-hot to chilly in a matter of days it didn't take a genius to realize that one was being fucked around. I just wished I had the nerve to demand to know what he was hiding from me.

The taxi finally pulled to a halt and Chad hurried around the side to pull open the door for me. He took my hand to help pull me to my feet, and kissed me again, as though he couldn't get enough of me. What in the ever-loving fuck was going on?

"What's all this in aid of?" I asked softly, but unable to stop myself from brushing my nose against his. Even now, when I stood at the end of the road with him, my body wanted to enjoy the last few moments before I took off for home. Even though it physically devastated me to think about walking away from this man, from the only man who had ever made me feel as though he truly wanted me, I knew I was going to do it no matter what.

"You'll see," he replied, and turned me towards the building we were parked outside. I glanced over, and my jaw dropped.

"Is that the place you took me...?"

"On your first night here," he nodded, a smile spreading over his face. "The very same."

"I can't believe you'd do this," I gasped. "I didn't even think you'd remember..."

"I remember everything with you, baby," he replied, slipping an arm around my waist.

I felt my resolve begin to waver. He'd put so much thought and effort into tonight; maybe what had happened before had just been a blip? I felt a wriggle in my stomach, obviously imaginary, it was only the size of a pea, but it made my hand move to my stomach protectively. I felt sad as I thought of the baby growing inside me, the baby that we had made together, and I wondered if I should stick around a little longer, and not to be so hasty in ending this relationship. I mean, technically, he had done nothing wrong. It could all be my own paranoia.

I let him lead me inside, biting my lip as I looked around. I remembered the way it had felt to see all those women so blatantly coming on to my man. How insecure I'd felt. It had started here. The sensation that the carpet could be pulled out from underneath me. The fear that one day one of those beautiful, perfect, bold women who came up to him for his attention or his autograph was going to turn his head.

The host led us to our table, and I was surprised when she took us to a small two-seater on the balcony. There was no-one else out there, just the two of us. As he pulled out my chair for me, he reached down to brush a strand of hair back from my neck as he did so. His fingertips traced over my skin and made me shiver. I clasped my hands tightly in my lap and tried not to focus on it.

"How did you get this seat?" My voice sounded shaky and small.

"I just wanted to make sure that we weren't disturbed," he replied softly, before planting a quick kiss where his fingers had just been.

I closed my eyes, and savored the smell of his aftershave, the warmth of his skin and the sensation of him standing so close to me. I wanted more, even though I knew I shouldn't, even though I had come out on this date with one thing, and one thing alone, on my mind. To break it off and leave, to give him the space he needed to make a decision that was bigger than either of us.

I unclasped my hands and let one lay on the tablecloth.

He sat down opposite me, and reached out to take my hand in his. Even though the water was shimmering in the late evening light beside us and looked very beautiful, I couldn't take my eyes off him. He still took my breath away. I had never laid eyes on a more handsome man and I knew I never would again.

Nervousness flickered across his face suddenly and my stomach dropped.

God, was he going to beat me to it, and break up with me? I stared him trying to hide the horror in my chest as his mouth opened.

"Madison," he began slowly, speaking every syllable of my name. "Madison, there's something I've been really wanting to tell you these last few weeks."

"Yeah?" I prompted him, voice so tiny that I was surprised he could hear me at all.

"I know I've been away from home a lot, babe, but I've been doing a lot of thinking about the two of us," he went on, and I noticed a tiny shake in his voice. This was not how people broke up, was it? I stared at him, unable to reply, a flicker of hope starting to ignite, silently urging him on.

He closed his eyes for a moment and smiled, as if he couldn't contain his joy. "But I'm ready to retire. I'm done with dancing. I just want to be with you now."

"But your contract—"

"It's all taken care of," he waved his hand. "I'm a free man now, Madison. I'm going to have a hell of a lot of time to spare. And I want to spend it with you."

"Chad, what are you saying?" My jaw hung open. This couldn't be going where I thought it was going.

Suddenly, the doors behind us sprang open, and I turned to the commotion. And my lips parted and I let out a squeak of surprise when I saw who it was.

"What the hell are they doing here!" I exclaimed, as a half-dozen of Chad's dancers spilled out onto the deck with us. From speakers somewhere above us, music started to play, music I recognized. It was playing the first time Chad and I met, when he had called me up on stage in London. I turned and gaped at him, waiting for him to explain what in the name of hell was going on, but he just shrugged and mouthed, "Enjoy the show."

He joined his mates and they all began to move in time with the beat, in perfect harmony, but there was only one person I could see. It was like my vision had narrowed in on Chad, like no-one else in the world mattered but him. The music dulled slightly in my ears as he stepped towards me, and then, to my utter shock, dropped to one knee in front of me.

"Madison," he took my hand as he dipped his other one into the pocket of his blazer. "I know this is a bit soon, but there's something I want to ask you."

"Chad..." I gasped, shaking like a leaf with joy and excitement. This couldn't be happening. All that distance, all that worry, and this was what he had been planning all along?

"Madison, I love you," he said, his voice, so loud it was as though he wanted the whole restaurant, the whole city, to know. "And I can't imagine my life without you. I have big changes ahead of me, and I want you there by my side the whole time."

He pulled out a box from his jacket and popped it open, revealing a ring that glimmered like the ocean beyond us.

"Will you marry me?"

For a moment, I forgot that I was meant to come up with an answer. Thoughts were rushing through my head, so fast I couldn't keep them straight. But then my eyes met his and my eyes filled with tears. What did he expect me to say? He'd always had my heart. From the first moment he looked into my eyes in that sea of women.

"I love you too," I breathed. "And, yes. Of course, I will."

There was a spontaneous burst of applause from inside the restaurant as he slipped the ring over my finger and grabbed me and kissed me. I held on to him tightly, never wanting to let go, my fingers digging into his flesh like I wanted to leave an impression on his skin. When he pulled back, he had the biggest smile on his face, and I grinned back. Happier than I had ever been in my whole life.

"I think you can give us a little privacy now, guys." He glanced over to his dancers, all of whom quickly filed out to leave us by ourselves once more. Some of them gave him a slap on the back, or offered up congratulations of some kind before they went. Then before I knew it, I was alone again with my fiancé.

My fiancé. I couldn't stop running the word around in my head, trying to make it stick.

I glanced at the restaurant, where a bunch of people were still watching us and smiling. A couple were even recording the whole thing. No doubt it will be on YouTube by tomorrow.

Chad sat down opposite me. "I think that should do to keep any women away, right?" he remarked dryly.

I laughed. All my worries felt like a million miles away now, and I was struggling to remember why I'd been so hung up on it in the first place. Chad was mine, and he wanted the whole world to know. I couldn't think of anything more romantic than that.

"I think it should," I agreed, then took a deep breath. He had surprised me, and now it was time for me to do the same to him. Now that I knew he actually wanted to be with me, there was no reason to hold back on giving him the good news.

"There's something I need to tell you," I admitted, leaning in close; his brow furrowed.

"You really want to do this, right?" he asked, suddenly nervous.

"More than anything," I assured him, nodding vigorously. "It's just…there's something else, too."

"Then what is it?"

I stared at him, into the eyes of the man I loved, and tried to commit this moment to memory, the last moment before everything would change forever.

"I'm pregnant."

The words hung in the air between us for a moment as he

simply gazed at me, his mouth slightly agape with shock. My heart was pounding in my chest, and I prayed that this wasn't going to scare him off. Sure, he had proposed, but this baby was a whole other step forward, one that he hadn't accounted for yet. Oh God! Maybe he wasn't ready for this…

"You're serious?" he whispered.

I could feel myself drop from the high I had been feeling. What was I going to do if he didn't want the baby? I was keeping it no matter what. "Yes," I whispered back.

He shook his head as if he couldn't believe his ears. "This is incredible."

"I plan to keep it," I croaked.

Suddenly, he leaned over and kissed me. When he pulled back, he actually let out a whoop of excitement. "You plan to keep it. What the hell? It's ours, not just yours."

I was too overcome with relief. He wanted the baby!

"When did you find out?" he demanded, the smile practically cracking his face in two.

"Yesterday," I admitted, the words pouring out of me, like I had unstopped a cork. I was just so glad to finally be telling him the truth about all of it, after keeping it from him from what felt like a lifetime. "I wanted to keep it, but I wasn't sure if you did…"

"Of course, I want to have it. How could you even think anything else?" He kissed me again, and then laughed loudly. "This is perfect. Just perfect."

"Yeah, it really is," I beamed across the table at him. It was odd to think that only a half-hour ago I had been sure this evening would end with me splitting up with him, and now I was sitting here, a ring glimmering on my finger, his baby inside me, and knowing that he wanted nothing more than to stick this out with me. "But I am a bit scared."

He frowned. "Scared?"

"Our future. What happens now?" I asked.

Chad took my hand and brought me right back down to earth with a smile. "We have an amazing dinner together," he began, tracing his fingers over my knuckles. "Then we go home and ... celebrate, properly. Without an audience."

I grinned. "Okay..."

"Don't worry. I'm here all the way to the finish line. We'll make plans. We'll take a day at a time and no matter what happens we'll have each other, but for now, let's just enjoy our dinner."

"Perfect," I beamed at him, and I meant it. I couldn't think of anything I wanted to do more in the world than spend the rest of the evening with him, my future husband, the father of my child, the most important man in the world to me.

CHAPTER 29

EPILOGUE

MADISON

"How's Nathan?" Chad asked as I made my way back out to the beach. I took up my place on the golden sand next to him, and tipped my head back to let the sun soak into my face.

"Sleeping," I replied, letting out a long sigh of relief. "At last." I looked out over the glittering water beyond us, and once again had to remind myself that this was real life. This was really my home, in Miami, with Chad. In a lovely house a little outside the city so that we could raise our son away from the hustle and bustle of the urban life.

He had surprised me with it when we had come back from our honeymoon. I still had no idea how he'd found the time to build something like this behind my back, but he had taken in every single one of my comments and ideas about the kind of place I wanted to live in, and turned them into our reality. A reality with a stretch of private beach and plenty of guest rooms so that my family could come over and visit whenever they wanted.

"He always goes down right away when I'm the one putting him to sleep," he teased. "He must like me better."

"Uh, uh, no way, he's going to be a total Mommy's boy," I shot back, as I reached for the mojito Chad had made up for me.

"Yeah? We'll see about that. I'm not having no son of mine hanging onto your skirts. I'm the only one who'll be doing that," he mocked, reaching over to skim his fingers up my bare arm.

"I was referring to how much control each of us has," I replied primly. "As far as I can see Nathan walks all over you."

"No, he doesn't."

"Yes, he does. You won't tell him off for anything."

"Yes, I do."

I settled myself more comfortably on the sand. "We'll have Sasha judge when she comes over next month."

"That's doesn't sound very fair. She's your sister."

"Yeah, but she's basically made it clear that she likes you more than me," I reminded. "You remember the wedding?"

"In all fairness, she had had a couple of drinks by then."

"And I've seen her drunk plenty of times, and she never got up and gave a speech about how much she loved any of my boyfriends," I told him. "Trust me, she likes you."

"Well, I can't help it if I'm charming."" Flashing his most charming smile, he rolled over to give me that look.

I raised my eyebrows at him. "Stop it."

He cocked his head at me. "What?"

I rolled my eyes. "Oh, come on. You know what."

"I'm not allowed to think about how hot my wife looks in a bikini?" he asked, playing innocent.

"I think the only reason you got the private beach on this place was so you could ogle me in bikinis every chance you got," I faux-scolded him. "I thought you would have gotten your fill last night."

"Not a chance," he said, and he went to touch me again, but I pulled away from him playfully. He grinned again. "What's this now?" he asked, his voice dropping to a low growl, letting me know that he was up for whatever game that I wanted to play.

I took another sip of my drink, letting the cool, minty freshness spread over my tongue. A year ago, I might have needed the alcohol to have the confidence to do what I was about to do, but right now, all I needed was the way he was looking at me. I got to my feet, turned away from him, and slowly swayed my hips back and forth as I reached up to undo the tie that held up my bikini top. I had to go up a size in everything above the waist after the pregnancy, and my boobs still hadn't gone down, but I certainly wasn't complaining. And by the look in his eyes, neither was he.

His eyes never left me as I slowly peeled off my top, and then sensuously hooked my fingers under the hips of my bikini bottoms. I slipped the scrap of cloth down slowly, stepping out of them one at a time. Then I turned around and stretched my arms up over my head, as though I was oh-so-casually stripping down and I didn't even know he was there.

I smiled inwardly when I heard a growl escape his mouth.

Suddenly he was behind me, sliding his hands around my middle and pulling me against him. His body had softened slightly in the few months he'd been away from dancing, but I was pretty sure I preferred it this way. It reminded me that he was mine now, all mine, that he had committed his life to me and that he didn't spend evenings grinding up on other women. I mean, yeah, sometimes I still got him to put on a show for me, but that was the extent of his dancing days.

He kissed my neck softly, and I closed my eyes.

"I want to make another baby with you," he purred into my ear.

I felt my knees begin to buckle a little out from beneath me. It was the sexiest thing he could have come out with right then. Ever since Nathan had come along three months ago, I hadn't been able to stop talking about having another kid. I adored our son so much, and the house had so much sprawling space that all I wanted to do was fill it with dozens of little Chads and Madisons.

"Mmm, don't tempt me," I replied, turning and wrapping my arms around him. He kissed me on the mouth, a sweet, tender smooch that made my heart race. I couldn't believe that this man was my husband. Before him, I had always imagined the word depicting some rotund man sitting in front of the TV, drinking beer.

But Chad was nothing like that.

He was intimately involved in Nathan's upbringing, focused on getting his dance studio off the ground, and flatteringly committed to me. Nothing seemed to slow him down; in fact, retiring from dancing only seemed to give him more motivation to do everything else he had always wanted to with his life.

He guided me down to the sand, pulling me on top of him. I ran my hands over his chest and down his stomach, undoing the tie of his trunks and pulling them down his body in one motion. He was already rock hard, and I wrapped my fingers around his length and stroked him a couple of times. Watching me he ran his fingers over my thighs and sighed with pleasure. I swayed back and forth a little, knowing that he liked the way my body moved when I was on top of him like this.

"I need to be inside you, like, right now," he ordered, reaching up to trace his thumb over my bottom lip. I shifted forward, needing no more encouragement, and lowered myself down on his cock.

"Fuck," he groaned, loudly enough that I instinctively shot a look up at the house. Once a mother always a mother, but there was really no need. Nathan slept like a dream, and wouldn't have even heard us if we'd both been screaming the place down. Which I had to admit, I had done in the past.

I began to move slowly, back and forth, planting my hands on his chest for support, and I thought about what he'd said before – how he wanted to make another baby with me, wanted to expand this family of ours. I closed my eyes and tipped my head back, the intense intimacy of those state-ments flooding my body with need for him, need that he was only too happy to fulfill. He thrust up into me, holding my hips steady, moving hard and deep. He knew never to hold back when it came to us; I had fucked him dozens of times like this, and every time it felt as though he moved a little deeper, a little rougher. I liked it.

The sound of our fevered breath mingled with the sound of the ocean behind us. Time seemed to drop away as I rocked back and forth on top of him. I needed this. Even though we fucked practically every day, I still craved him with a hunger that I wasn't sure would ever drop away.

When I had first laid eyes on him, on that stage more than a year ago, I never could have imagined what I had felt was so true. That the connection would never really be severed, or even decrease in intensity with time. He stroked my clit, and my head tipped back. I was so close. So close. Suddenly he sat up, ran his tongue over my throat and plunged himself as far inside me as he could manage. The shock of the sensation was enough to make me come all at once, my body trembling as the bubble of pleasure ballooned inside me and burst out of my mouth.

"Ah!" I cried, the sound whipped away by the soft breeze coming off the water.

He came moments later, holding me close and steady as he exploded inside me. God, I would never get over how good it felt to have him fuck me without a condom, the closeness was incomparable to anything I'd experienced before.

We pulled apart and he kissed me long and sweet, taking my breath away. I would have been happy staying there for the rest of the day, but unfortunately, I had things to do.

"I have a meeting with a client in twenty minutes," I reminded, reluctantly pulling away. I never want our time together to end

"Yeah, I remember," he said with a sigh.

I slid off of him and went to grab my bikini. I was meeting with a potential new client about stepping in for their engagement photos; not a huge gig, but it was a start, since I had let my photography take a back seat in the midst of the wedding planning and having Nathan.

"I'll come in and keep an eye on Nathan," he said, getting to his feet and following me as I made my way into the house to get dressed.

"He's sleeping," I reminded him. "So please don't wake him up."

"I won't," he promised, as he slipped an arm around me and kissed me again. Like he couldn't resist me. He was still naked, and when I pulled back, it took everything I had not to drag him into our bedroom right there and then.

"You're intent on distracting me today, aren't you?" I scolded playfully.

"Just want you to walk into your meeting with a smile on your face," he replied with a cocky grin.

"That you have definitely done." I kissed him on the corner of his mouth and went to pull on some clothes from the generous walk-in wardrobe he'd built especially for me.

"Later," He called over his shoulder as he went to tend to Nathan.

There was a big smile on my face as I turned to watch my husband's tight butt as he walked away to take care of our son. I could never have imagined this life for myself, but now that I was here, it seemed utterly, perfectly obvious that I was living in paradise.

The End

COMING SOON

THE RIVAL

CHAPTER 1

SIENNA

There are people who drag their butts into the office on Monday morning, then spend the next five days looking forward to Friday evening.

I'm not one of them.

I don't just work Monday through Friday. Often, I'll work right through the weekend. And I freaking love it. I honestly do. I'm a career girl and I love my job. To me, work is such a huge part of my life that it is quite literally my whole life.

"Good morning," I greet, a bright smile plastered on my face as I breeze through the open-floorplan layout of Dunhurst Real Estate. It reminds me of a beehive, so many cubicles attached to one another, so much buzzing among the worker bees.

One day, I'll have the corner office. I glance longingly at it every morning on my way to the cubicle-with-a-door which currently passes for my office. I suppose I should be grateful. At least it has a door, and high walls to give me privacy. Most people don't even have that much.

I reach my door without getting pulled into random conversations about the weather, or questions about what I did during the weekend. That's always a pointless question, anyway. Everybody knows what I do with my time. I work. Maybe they're hoping I'll mix things up and talk about a great party, or recommend a movie I went to.

But how is a person supposed to hit their sales goals when they spend their weekends partying, going to brunch and the movies, or generally being slack? Whenever I overhear complaints from one of my coworkers about middling sales, I have to bite my tongue to keep from bringing this up.

If you want something great, you have to be willing to sacrifice the not-so-great stuff. It's all a matter of choices. Sure, I'd love to be able to maintain my position in the company while enjoying a busy social life, but that's not possible. It is what it is.

Closing my office door, I can hang up my coat on the rack in the corner, and sit down to plan my day. Call me old-fashioned, but I believe in writing out my to-do lists at the start of every day. I can always add items to my ticker on the computer, but the act of writing it all down soothes me in a way technology simply can't. And it's an excuse to put down my phone for a minute.

A very, very rare minute for me.

"Call Cindy," I murmur, scrawling the name of one of my recently closed clients. I like to check in a week or so after closing to see how things are going with the new house, maybe send a gift basket or flowers. I add a sub-note beneath that to remind myself to place an order. I have other such calls to make after that, seeing as how I've sold four additional properties in the last month.

It's been busy. God, I love it.

A knock at my door makes my nose wrinkle. Can't they give me ten minutes of peace? "Yes?" I call out, forcing the irritation out of my voice.

Becca pokes her head in, her cloud of auburn curls making an appearance before she does. I wish I had hair as pretty as hers, but I know I'd never be able to get it to behave as well as hers. I'd probably end up a frizzy mess, forced to eternally wear a messy bun. Who has the time?

"Rodney's looking for you," she whispers before wincing.

My eyes dart over to my phone, checking the time. "Not even nine-fifteen yet? It must be my lucky day."

"Godspeed." She hurries off, probably grateful she's not the one the boss wants to see this early on a Monday. I can only imagine what he wants from me at this time of the morning.

Rodney's not bad, as far as bosses go. I worked for some real winners throughout college, during my internship and in the year following that. Rodney's intense, sure, and a hard worker, I mean, how else would he get to be in the corner office? But he rewards good work and doles out opportunities to those he knows will make the most of them.

I hope that's what this is about.

I take a quick look at myself in my compact. My chocolate-brown hair is in place, smoothed back in its low ponytail. I really do wish I had more time to make it look nicer, but even when I try, it never comes out the way I'd like. The makeup around my hazel eyes looks good. I didn't smudge it on the way here.

I stand and smooth down the skirt of my black dress before striding out into the beehive. This could be good. No, this *will* be good. He's going to congratulate me on my sales last month. He's going to give me a raise. He's going to give me a new listing. He's going to…

The sight of an unwelcome presence outside his office door nearly stops me in my tracks.

Ugh.

Zack?

He would have to stop in for a moment of the boss's time when I'm on my way in for something I've decided must be very, very important. This is so like him, acting as if the entire world revolves around him and what he wants. Forget the rest of us, forget having a little consideration of his boss's time first thing on a Monday.

The thing is, he acts that way because people treat him as though it's okay to be an inconsiderate jerk. Just because he's good looking, the women around the office fawn over him like he's the second coming. I guess that sort of drop dead gorgeousness will breed confidence throughout other areas of life too. Not that I'm ugly or anything, just that he's in a class by himself. Even I can admit that, and I can't stand the man.

Why?

Because he's almost as good as me. Maybe as good as, certainly not better than. To date he is my only competition in the company. The only agent who closes nearly as many properties as I do, for around as much money as I do.

All right. He had a slightly higher sales figure than I did last month, but only by a few measly hundred thousand dollars. That's nothing when you're selling the sort of luxury properties we handle.

Damn it, he's making a move to close Rodney's office door behind him. I put on a little speed, hurrying the rest of the way in order to catch the door before it swings shut.

"Excuse me," I murmur through gritted teeth. "I was told Rodney wanted to see me."

His ice blue eyes size me up, and one corner of his mouth quirks up in a smile. "Small world. So was I."

We both turn to our boss, who's seated behind his desk. As always, the office is pristine, without so much as a single paper or pen out of place. Not a single speck of dust anywhere. He's a very deliberate man, Rodney is.

If this were my office, I would be the same way.

He flashes us one of his million-dollar smiles, the sort of smile I'm still working on, the one that closes never ending, multi-million-dollar sales. "I wanted to see the both of you at once, as a matter of fact. Please, close the door and have a seat."

I exchange a look with Zack—for once, the two of us are in the same boat, both slightly confused and feeling as though we're about to go up in front of a firing squad. But if he can be confident, so can I. I close the door and walk over to one of the chairs which face Rodney's side of the desk, taking a seat and folding my hands in my lap.

He hasn't stopped smiling, looking for all the world like the cat that ate the canary. He has News for us, the sort of news that requires a capital-N when I imagine it in my head. I've seen that gleam in his eyes before. And it wasn't good the last time.

"We don't have much time, so I'll give you the Reader's Digest version: Nick McMann is selling his estate, and he's going with Dunhurst for the sale."

My mind immediately starts to race. The McMann property is legendary, built with the sort of money only a multi-platinum selling recording artist can afford to spend. I can see it in my head. It looks like something from that old TV show, *Dynasty*, somewhat more modern, but just as sprawling and over-the-top.

And he's going with us to close the sale.

I have a feeling I know why Rodney called us in, and I'm more than up to the challenge. He wants to see which of the two of us can close it first. No freaking contest. I already have a half-dozen people in mind to call up and see if they're interested.

A quick glance out of the corner of my eye tells me Zack's thinking along the same lines. He can't hide that wolfish smile he gets on his stupid face whenever he sees himself close to a big sale. I wonder how he manages to sell anything at all, seeing as how he gives away what he's thinking with that stupid, arrogant smile of his.

I'm gonna wipe the floor with him.

"We're talking the sale of the decade here," Rodney continues, oblivious to the silent war going on between his staff. As far as he's concerned, Zack and I are his two shining stars. I don't think he would care even if he knew we hate each other, so long as we keep making money for the company.

"No kidding," Zack observes with a smarmy grin. God, he is such an ass kisser.

"There's just one little catch." Rodney's smile fades. "It has to be closed within a week."

"What?" I realize a moment later that Zack said it just as I did. For once, something has managed to knock him off his high horse. He looks just as shook as I feel.

Rodney holds up his hands, signaling silence before the two of us can continue to work ourselves into a frenzy. A week? Is he insane? "It's the only stipulation Nick has. He wants the sale finalized in a week. He's moving out of the country and doesn't want any loose ends."

"A week? He's crazy," I mutter. Just like a clueless celebrity. He obviously doesn't understand or doesn't care about how much work goes into a sale, especially a high-profile sale like this one. They think we can just snap our fingers and make magic happen.

"If there's anyone I trust to get this done, it's the two of you."

Silence. He is greeted by complete silence for at least five seconds after dropping that adorable little bombshell on our heads. I'm still reeling from the timeline situation, and he goes and adds this to the mix.

"The two of us?" Zack croaks.

I can't help but feel slightly pleased at his incredulity, even though I know it comes from the fact that he likes me around him as much as I like do. Which is to say, not even a little bit.

Meanwhile, I'm too gobsmacked to speak. What is there to say? To argue with him would make me look childish, and I know Rodney well enough by now to know he doesn't change his mind once he's made it up. I can only sit here and absorb whatever it is he has to say.

"The two of you," he confirms, smiling again. "You're the two best salespeople I have, which shouldn't be a surprise to either of you. I couldn't trust anyone, but you guys to do this. Let's face it: this will be a challenge, and a big one so I would rather have two great minds on it than only one. And considering the price Nick's looking to pull down, your commission will be sizable even when split in half."

Zack looks like somebody just killed his dog.

I feel like somebody just killed mine. If I had one, that is. This isn't going to go well. I can't believe Rodney would do this—high-profile sale or not. The fact that he doesn't have enough faith in me to let me handle it on my own speaks volumes. I'm not a child. I don't need my hand held.

And I sure as hell don't need Zack sliming his way around the place, doing little work and taking all the credit for what's surely going to be my sale. I've never exactly had a lot of respect for people who charm their way through life without actually working for anything, which is exactly the sort of guy he is.

"Off you go, then. You both have a lot of work to do. Becca should have all the preliminary information together for you by now." When he turns to face his laptop, I know we've been dismissed for good. No chance of changing his mind, no way to beg him to reconsider without looking like a whiny little crybaby.

My knees are shaking as I stand, but I do my best to cover up the absolute fury roiling in my stomach as I walk out with Zack behind me. There are times when even the biggest sale and tastiest commission aren't worth it. I hope this isn't one of those times, but something tells me it will be.

No wonder people hate Mondays so much. I think I might start hating them, too.

CHAPTER 2

ZACK

He's got to be kidding. Even as I walk out of the door I keep waiting for him to yell "Gotcha!" or something like that, but he hasn't. Yet. I'm afraid he never will. I'm afraid he seriously means to pair us together.

Her? He wants me to work with the ice princess? Doesn't he know what an insufferable little bitch she is? And that's not me being mean. Hell, everybody in the office thinks so. They're just too afraid of her, and of the way Rodney obviously loves her, to say anything about it. She's one of the two top agents in the company.

I just happen to be the other one.

If Rodney wasn't such a stickler for keeping everybody accountable by making us work like bees in a hive, there would be three offices on our floor instead of only his. Mine would be one of them, and hers would be the other one. Even I can admit she's damn good at what she does.

Why does she have to be such a hard-nosed bitch about it,

though? That's what I don't get. All she cares about is work, all she wants is the sale. Forget making friends in the office, forget being a human being and not some robot who understands nothing but numbers and commissions. There isn't even any making small talk with her. She can't even be bothered to take time out of her busy day around the coffee maker, the way civilized people do when they work together.

There's a reason I steer clear of her and anybody like her, male or female. Especially when they happen to be my competition.

But now Rodney has gone and dropped her in my fucking lap and asked me to play nice. We have to be a team. I've never been good at acting as though I like someone when I don't. And I don't have a reputation for playing nice.

What a hell of a week this is going to be.

I follow her out of Rodney's office and wish she wasn't wearing that tight dress. It's not enough that I have to work with her. I have to watch that cute little ass wiggling back and forth every time she walks past.

I know I don't technically have to watch. I just can't help it. Why does she have to be so… her?

It's not like I've ever had trouble with women—far from it. Even now, I catch three passing coworkers checking me out. I'm used to it. I'm not being big-headed. It's just a fact of life. If I decided I wanted a little company tonight, it wouldn't be too hard to convince any of the single women in the office to join me.

My gaze drops to the straight set of shoulders marching

ahead of me. But this one. This Sienna. She acts like she's untouchable, like she has no time for anything as basic as sexual needs. She's so far above mere mortals like me. That's probably my biggest problem with her.

We reach her wannabe office first, as mine is at the other end of the floor. Thank God, I'm not checking her ass out anymore when she stops suddenly and turns around to glare at me. I don't need her accusing me of harassment.

She sighs, like she's the only one with a problem. I barely manage to hold my tongue to keep from asking if I'm making her late for the surgery to get the stick removed from her ass.

"I guess we should take some time to go over a plan for this," she says, making sure to sound as bored as possible.

"Yes, I guess so. I should be able to clear some time today."

Her eyes roll. It's clearly a gesture she's practiced throughout her life. "Dinner tonight. I'll send you a calendar request. We can talk it over then."

"I can hardly wait."

She rewards me with another eye roll before stepping into her makeshift office and closing the door with a decisive snap of the latch.

She'd better not plan on acting that way throughout our time together, but something tells me she will. She'll make me feel like this is the ultimate inconvenience. Like she's supremely put out by this. She has to be the most self-centered person I've ever met.

Which is saying something, because I've known my share.

Without warning and completely inappropriately, an image of her sour mouth wrapped around my cock slips into my head, and immediately my cock twitches with interest.

Fuck!

I jam my fists into my pants pockets and continue to my desk, grateful she can't see the way she's affected me. It would be a power trip for her to know I'm secretly lusting after her. Which is extremely annoying because I don't usually react to women like this and I don't like showing my hand so easily. Especially not to someone like her. How am I supposed to rush through this job and still do it the right way when she's part of it?

At least I have a door to close behind me, shutting out the rest of the office for a while. They don't need to see me sitting here with my head in my hands. It would ruin the image I've put together over the years.

I guess I have no choice. I can't refuse Rodney. I need this sale. Not for the commission. She's welcome to it all if she'll just let me take the credit for it. I have my reasons for needing this sale on my resume and it's nothing to do with money. Worst part is, I know I could close this sale on my own. No point asking her to let me make the sale on my own in exchange for all the commission. Knowing the way she is, she'll want to take all the credit, all the commission, and my head on a platter.

There's got to be a way to get around this mess.

An idea starts to bloom in my mind, one which probably isn't completely fair, but hey, all's fair in love and war and real estate. I don't feel too bad about it as I'll let her keep all the commission.

Anyway, instinct tells me she'd do the same to me if she had enough imagination.

The Rival will be out next month.

www.ingramcontent.com/pod-product-compliance
Lightning Source LLC
Chambersburg PA
CBHW021144130626
46554CB00005B/1662